W9-BTJ-062

"I'm asking you to be my guest for the evening. But it is up to you, Rosa. Clearly you planned on going to a party tonight."

Vittorio eased the mask from her fingers. "Why should you miss out on the biggest night of Carnevale just because you became separated from your friends?"

He could tell she was tempted, could all but taste her excitement about being handed a lifeline to an evening she'd all but given up on, even while the questions and misgivings swirled in the depths of her eyes.

He smiled. He knew how to turn on the charm when the need arose, whether he was involved in negotiations with a foreign diplomat or romancing a woman. "Serendipity," he repeated. "A happy chance, for both of us."

Her eyes lifted to meet his. Long-lashed, shy eyes filled with uncertainty and nerves, and again, he was struck by her air of vulnerability. She was very different to the women he usually met.

"Thank you," she said.

"Is that a yes?"

She took a deep breath before giving a decisive nod with her own tentative smile.

Passion in Paradise

Exotic escapes...and red-hot romances!

Step into a jet-set world where first class is the *only* way to travel. From Madrid to Venice, you'll find a billionaire at every turn! But no billionaire is complete without the perfect romance. Especially when that passion is found in the most incredible destinations...

Find out what happens in:

Wedding Night Reunion in Greece by Annie West

A Scandalous Midnight in Madrid by Susan Stephens

His Shock Marriage in Greece by Jane Porter

Available now!

Consequences of a Hot Havana Night by Louise Fuller

Coming soon!

And look out for more Passion in Paradise stories!

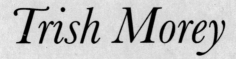

Trish Morey

PRINCE'S VIRGIN
IN VENICE

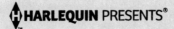

HARLEQUIN PRESENTS®

If you purchased this book without a cover you should be aware
that this book is stolen property. It was reported as "unsold and
destroyed" to the publisher, and neither the author nor the
publisher has received any payment for this "stripped book."

Recycling programs
for this product may
not exist in your area.

ISBN-13: 978-1-335-53856-7

Prince's Virgin in Venice

First North American publication 2019

Copyright © 2019 by Trish Morey

All rights reserved. Except for use in any review, the reproduction or
utilization of this work in whole or in part in any form by any electronic,
mechanical or other means, now known or hereafter invented, including
xerography, photocopying and recording, or in any information storage
or retrieval system, is forbidden without the written permission of the
publisher, Harlequin Enterprises Limited, 22 Adelaide St. West, 40th Floor,
Toronto, Ontario M5H 4E3, Canada.

This is a work of fiction. Names, characters, places and incidents are
either the product of the author's imagination or are used fictitiously,
and any resemblance to actual persons, living or dead, business
establishments, events or locales is entirely coincidental.

This edition published by arrangement with Harlequin Books S.A.

For questions and comments about the quality of this book,
please contact us at CustomerService@Harlequin.com.

® and TM are trademarks of Harlequin Enterprises Limited or its
corporate affiliates. Trademarks indicated with ® are registered in the
United States Patent and Trademark Office, the Canadian Intellectual
Property Office and in other countries.

Printed in U.S.A.

Trish Morey always fancied herself a writer—so why she became a chartered accountant is anyone's guess! But once she'd found her true calling there was no turning back. Mother of four budding heroines and wife to one true-life hero, Trish lives in an idyllic region of South Australia. Is it any wonder she believes in happy-ever-afters?

Find her at trishmorey.com or Facebook.com/trish.morey.

Books by Trish Morey

Harlequin Presents

Bartering Her Innocence
A Price Worth Paying?

One Night With Consequences

Consequence of the Greek's Revenge

21st Century Bosses

Fiancée for One Night

Bound by His Ring

Secrets of Castillo del Arco

Desert Brothers

Duty and the Beast
The Sheikh's Last Gamble
Captive of Kadar
Shackled to the Sheikh

Visit the Author Profile page
at Harlequin.com for more titles.

To magical Venezia,
floating city of love and romance

CHAPTER ONE

PRINCE VITTORIO D'MARBURG of Andachstein was fed up. Bored. Even in Venice at the height of carnival season, even on his way to the most exclusive party of the festival, still the Playboy Prince couldn't ignore the overwhelming sense of frustration that permeated his skin and drilled straight down into his bones.

Or maybe it was just the icy pricks from the February pea soup fog needling his skin that were turning his thoughts from carnival to cynical. It was a fog that turned the magical city invisible, precisely when the *calles* and narrow bridges were more crowded than ever with waves of costumed partygoers surging to and fro, competing for the available space—brightly garbed men and women for whom the fog failed to dampen the air of excitement and the energy that accompanied Carnevale.

It was if the floating city had been let off a leash and, fog or no, it was going to party.

Vittorio cut a swathe through the endless tide of carnival-goers, his cloak swirling in his wake, his mood blackening with every step.

The thronging crowds somehow parted and

made way for him. He didn't think too much about it. Maybe it was his warrior costume—a coat of mail and blue leather dressed with chain and gold braid—or maybe it was his battle-ready demeanour. Either way, it was as if they could read the hostility in his eyes as he headed towards the most exclusive party of the night.

And they could all see his eyes. Vittorio had given up playing with disguises when he was a child. There'd been no point. Everyone had always known it was him behind the mask.

Before the ancient well in the square that housed the Palazzo de Marigaldi, Vittorio's long strides slowed. Ordinarily he would have been relieved to reach his destination and escape the exuberant crowds—*should* have been relieved— except for the fact that his father had all too gleefully shared the news in his latest call, just minutes earlier, that the Contessa Sirena Della Corte, daughter of one of his oldest friends, was opportunely going to be in attendance.

Vittorio snorted—just as he'd done when his father had told him.

Opportunely.

He doubted it.

Opportunistically would no doubt be a better word. The woman was a human viper draped in designer artistry, lying in wait for a royal title— which marriage to him would bestow upon her.

And his father, despite Vittorio's blanket protests, had encouraged her to pursue her desperate ambition.

Little wonder Vittorio was in no hurry to get there.

Little wonder that, despite the assurances he'd made to his old friend Marcello that nothing would stop him attending his party tonight, Vittorio's enthusiasm had been on the wane ever since his father's call had come through.

Dio.

He'd come to Venice thinking the famous carnival would offer an escape from the stultifying atmosphere of the palace and the endless demands of the aging Prince Guglielmo, but it seemed they had stalked him here—along with the Contessa Sirena.

His father's choice for his next bride.

But after the experience of his first doomed marriage Vittorio wasn't about to be dictated to again—not when it came to the woman who would share his marriage bed.

The crowds were thickening, party deadlines were calling, and their excitement was at odds with his own dark thoughts. He was a man out of place, out of time. He was a man who had the world at his feet, and destiny snapping at his heels. He was a man who wanted to be able to make his own choices, but he was cursed with the heritage of his birth and his need to satisfy others before he could entertain his own needs.

He all but turned to walk away—from his destiny as much as from the party. He wasn't in the mood for going another few rounds with Sirena— wasn't in the mood for her blatant attempts at seduction, the pouting, and the affected hurt when her all too obvious charms went ignored.

Except there was no question of his not going. Marcello was his oldest friend and Vittorio had promised him he would be there. Sirena would just have to keep on pouting.

But curse his father for encouraging the woman.

Something caught his eye. A flash of colour amongst the crowd, a static burst of vermilion amidst the moving parade of costumes and finery, a glimpse of a knee, down low, and a hint of an upturned angular jaw up high—like snatches of a portrait in oils when all around were hazy watercolours.

His eyes narrowed as he willed the surging crowd to part. Catching a glance of a dark waterfall of wavy hair over one shoulder when the crowd obliged, he saw the woman turn her masked face up to the bridge, moving her head frantically with every passing costume, scanning, searching through the short veil of black lace that masked the top half of her face.

She looked lost. Alone. A tourist, most likely, fallen victim to Venice's tangle of streets and canals.

He looked away. It wasn't his problem. He had somewhere to be, after all. And yet still his eyes scoured the square. Nobody looked as if they had lost someone and were searching for her. Nobody looked anywhere close to claiming her.

He glanced back, seeking her between richly decorated masks topped with elaborate wigs and feathers, their wearers resplendent in costumes that spoke of centuries long past, when men wore fitted breeches and women wore gowns with tight bodices spilling their plump white breasts. For a moment he couldn't find her, and thought her gone, until a group of Harlequins with jester hats ringing with bells passed. And then he saw her raise one hand to her painted mouth before seeming to sag before him.

He watched as she thumbed off the mask and shook her hair back on a sigh—the long hair that curled over one shoulder. She swept it back with one hand, and her cloak slipped down to reveal one bare shoulder and a satin gown riding low over one breast, before she shivered and hurriedly tucked herself back under the cover of the cloak.

She was lost.

Alone.

With the kind of innocent beauty and vulnerability that tugged at him.

And suddenly Vittorio didn't feel so bored any more.

CHAPTER TWO

LOST IN VENICE. Panic pumped loud and hard through Rosa Ciavarro's veins as she squeezed herself out of the flow of costumed crowds pouring over the bridge and found a rare patch of space by the side of the canal, trying to catch her breath and calm her racing heart. But nothing could calm her desperate eyes.

She peered through the lace of her veil, searching for a sign that would tell her where she was, but when she managed to make out the name of the square it meant nothing and offered no clue as to where she was. Scanning the passing crowds for any hint of recognition proved just as useless. It was pointless. Impossible to tell who was who when everyone was in costume.

Meanwhile the crowds continued to surge over the bridge: Harlequins and Columbinas, vampires and zombies. And why not zombies, when in the space of a few minutes her highly anticipated night had teetered over the edge from magical into nightmarish?

Panic settled into glum resignation as she turned her head up to the inky sky swirling with fog and clutched her own arms, sighing out a long breath of frustration that merely added more mist to the swirling fog. It was futile, and it was time she gave up searching and faced the truth.

She'd crossed too many bridges and turned too many corners in a vain attempt to catch up with her friends, and there was no chance they'd ever find each other now.

It was the last night of Carnevale, and the only party she'd been able to afford to go to, and instead she was lost and alone at the base of a fog-bound bridge somewhere in Venice.

Pointless.

Rosa pulled her thin cloak more tightly around her shoulders. *Dio*, it was cold. She stamped her feet against the stones of the pavement to warm her legs, wishing she'd had the sense to make herself something warmer than this flimsy gown with its bare shoulders and high-low hem. Something that better suited the season. Preferably something worn over thermals and lined with fur.

'You'll be dancing all night,' Chiara had protested when Rosa had suggested she dress for the winter weather. 'Take it from me, you'll roast if you wear anything more.'

But Rosa wasn't roasting now. The damp air wound cold fingers around her ankles and up her shins, seeking and sucking out what body warmth it could find. She was so very cold! And for the first time in too many years to remember she felt tears prick at the corners of her eyes.

She sniffed. She wasn't the type to cry. She'd grown up with three older brothers who would mercilessly tease her if she did. As a child, she'd stoically endured any number of bumps and scratches, skinned knees and grazed elbows when she'd insisted on accompanying them on their adventures.

She hadn't cried when her brothers had taught her to ride a bike that was too large for her, letting her go fast on a rocky road until she'd crashed into an ancient fig tree. She hadn't cried when they'd helped her climb that same tree and then all clambered down and run away, leaving her to pick her own tentative way down. She'd fallen the last few feet to the dusty ground, collecting more scratches and bumps. All wounds she'd endured without a whimper.

But she'd never before been separated from her friends and lost in the labyrinthine *calles* of Venice on the biggest party night of the year, without her ticket or any way to contact them. Surely even her brothers would understand if she shed a tear or two of frustration now?

Especially if they knew the hideous amount she'd spent on her ticket!

She closed her eyes and pulled her cloak tighter around her, feeling the icy bite of winter working its way into her bones as resignation gave way to remorse. She'd had such high hopes for tonight. A rare night off in the midst of Carnevale. A chance to pretend she *wasn't* just another hotel worker, cleaning up after the holidaymakers who poured into the city. A chance to be part of the celebrations instead of merely watching from the sidelines.

But so much money!

Such a waste!

Laughter rang out from the bridge, echoing in the foggy air above the lapping canal—laughter that could well be directed at her. Because there was nobody to blame for being in this predicament but herself.

It had seemed such a good idea when Chiara had offered to carry her phone and her ticket. After all, they were going to the same party. And it *had* been a good idea—right up until a host of angels sprouting ridiculously fat white wings had surged towards them across a narrow bridge and she'd been separated from her friends and forced backwards. By the time she'd managed to shoulder her way between the feathered wings and get back to the bridge Chiara and her friends had been swallowed up in the fog and the crowds and were nowhere in sight.

She'd raced across the bridge and along the crowded paths as best she could, trying to catch up, colliding with people wearing headdresses constructed from shells, or jester hats strung with bells, or ball gowns nearly the width of the narrow streets. But she was relatively new to Venice, and unsure of the way, and she'd crossed so many bridges—too many—that even if Chiara turned back how would she even know where to find her? She could have taken any number of wrong turns.

Useless.

She might as well go home to the tiny basement apartment she shared with Chiara—wherever that was. Surely even if it took her all night she would stumble across it eventually. With a final sigh, she reefed the mask from her face. She didn't need a lace veil over her eyes to make her job any more difficult. She didn't need a mask tonight, period. There would be no party for her tonight.

Her cloak slipped as she pushed her hair back, inadvertently exposing one shoulder to the frigid air. She shivered as she grappled with the slippery cloth and tucked herself back under what flimsy protection it offered against the cold.

She was bracing herself to fight her way back over the bridge and retrace her steps when she saw him. A man standing by the well in the centre of the square. A man in a costume of blue trimmed with gold. A tall man, broad-shouldered, with the bearing of a warrior.

A man who was staring right at her.

Electricity zapped a jagged line down her spine.

No. Not possible. She darted a look over her shoulder—because why should he be looking at *her*? But there was nothing behind her but the canal and a crumbling wall beyond.

She swallowed as she turned back, raising her eyes just enough to see that he was now walking purposefully towards her, and the crowd was almost scattering around him. Even across the gloom of the lamp-lit square the intent in his eyes sent adrenaline spiking in her blood.

Fight versus flight? There was no question of her response. She knew that whoever he was, and whatever he was thinking, she'd stayed there too long. And he was still moving, long strides bridging the distance between them, and still her feet refused to budge. She was anchored to the spot, when instead she should be pushing bodily into the bottleneck of people at the bridge and letting the crowd swallow her up and carry her away.

Much too soon he was before her, a man mountain of leather tunic and braid and chain, his shoulder-length hair loose around a face that spoke of power. A high brow above a broad nose and a jawline framed with steel and rendered in concrete, all hard lines and planes. And eyes of the most startling blue. Cobalt. No, he was no mere warrior. He must be a warlord. A god. He could be either.

Her mouth went dry as she looked up at him, but maybe that was just the heat that seemed to radiate from his body on this cold, foggy evening.

'Can I help you?' he said, in a voice as deep as he was tall.

He spoke in English, although with an accent that suggested he was not. Her heart was hammering in her chest, and her tongue seemed to have lost the ability to form words in any language.

He angled his head, his dark eyes narrowing. *'Vous-êtes perdu?'* he tried, speaking in French this time.

Her French was patchier than her English, so she didn't bother trying to respond in either. *'No parlo Francese,'* she said, sounding breathless even to her own ears——but how could she not sound breathless, standing before a man whose very presence seemed to suck the oxygen out of the misty air?

'You're Italian?' he said, in her own language this time.

'Si.' She swallowed, the action kicking up her chin. She tried to pretend it was a show of confidence, just like the challenge she did her best to infuse into her voice. 'Why were you watching me?'

'I was curious.'

She swallowed. She'd seen those women standing alone and waiting on the side of the road, and she had one idea why he might be curious about a woman standing by herself in a square.

She looked down at her gown, at the stockinged legs visible beneath the hem of her skirt. She knew she was supposed to look like a courtesan, but… 'This is a costume. I'm not—you know.'

One side of his mouth lifted—the slightest re-arrangement of the hard angles and planes of his face that turned his lips into an almost-smile, a change so dramatic that it took her completely by surprise.

'This is Carnevale. Nobody is who they seem tonight.'

'And who are you?'

'My name is Vittorio. And you are…?'

'Rosa.'

'Rosa,' he said, with the slightest inclination of his head.

It was all she could do not to sway at the way her name sounded in his rich, deep voice. It was the cold, she told herself, the slap of water against the side of the canal and the whisper of the fog against her skin, nothing more.

'It is a pleasure to meet you.'

He held out one hand and she regarded it warily. It was a big hand, with buckles cuffing sleeves that looked as if they would burst open if he clenched so much as a muscle.

'I promise it doesn't bite,' he said.

She looked up to see that the curve of his lips had moved up a notch and there was a glimmer of warmth in his impossibly blue eyes. And she didn't mind that he seemed to be laughing at her, because the action had worked some kind of miracle on his face, giving a glimpse of the man beneath the warrior. So he was mortal after all…not some god conjured up by the shifting fog.

Almost reluctantly she put her hand in his, then felt his fingers curl around her hers and heat bloom in her hand. It was a delicious heat that curled seductively into her bloodstream and stirred a response low down in her belly, a feeling so unexpected, so unfamiliar, that it sent alarm bells clanging in her brain.

'I have to go,' she said, pulling her hand from his, feeling the loss of his body heat as if it had been suctioned from her flesh.

'Where do you have to go?'

She looked over her shoulder at the bridge. The crowds were thinning now, most people having arrived at their destinations, and only latecomers were still rushing. If she set off now, at least she'd have a chance of getting herself warm.

'I'm supposed to be somewhere. A party.'

'Do you know where this party is?'

'I'll find it,' she said, with a conviction she didn't feel.

Because she had no idea where she was or where the party was, and because even if she did by some miracle manage to find the party there was the slight matter of an entry ticket no longer in her possession.

'You haven't a clue where it is or how to get there.'

She looked back at him, ready to snap a denial, but his eyes had joined with his lips and there was no mistaking that he'd know she was lying.

She pulled her cloak tighter around her and kicked up her chin. 'What's it to you?'

'Nothing. It's not a crime. Some would say that in Venice getting lost is compulsory.'

She bit her tongue as she shivered under her cloak.

Maybe if you hadn't dropped more money than you could spare on a ticket, and maybe if you had a phone with working GPS, you wouldn't mind getting lost in Venice.

'You're cold,' he said, and before she could deny it or protest he had undone the chain at his neck and swung his cloak around her shoulders.

Her first instinct was to protest. New to city life she might be, but in spite of what he'd said she wasn't naïve enough to believe that this man's offer of help came without strings. But his cloak was heavy and deliciously warm, the leather supple and infused with a masculine scent. The scent of *him*. She breathed it in, relishing the blend of leather and man, rich and spiced, and her protest died on her lips. It was so good to feel snug.

'*Grazie,*' she said, warmth enveloping her, spreading to legs that felt as if they'd been chilled for ever. Just for a minute she would take this warmth, use it to defrost her blood and re-energise her deflated body and soul, and then she'd insist she was fine, give his cloak back and try to find her way home.

'Is there someone you can call?'

'I don't have my phone.' She looked down at the mask in her hands, feeling stupid.

'Can I call someone for you?' he asked, pulling a phone from a pouch on his belt.

For a moment Rosa felt a glimmer of hope. But only for a moment. Because Chiara's phone number was logged in her phone's memory, but not in her own. She shook her head, the tiny faint hope snuffed out. Her Carnevale was over before it had even begun.

'I don't know the number. It's programmed into my phone, but…'

He dropped the phone back in its pouch. 'You don't know where this party is?'

Suddenly she was tired. Worn out by the rollercoaster of emotions, weary of questions that exposed how unprepared and foolish she'd been. This stranger might be trying to help, and he might be right when he assumed she didn't know where the party was—he *was* right—but she didn't need a post-mortem. She just wanted to go back to her apartment and her bed, pull the covers over her head and forget this night had ever happened.

'Look, thanks for your help. But don't you have somewhere to be?'

'I do.'

She cocked an eyebrow at him in challenge. 'Well, then?'

A gondola slipped almost silently along the canal behind her. Fog swirled around and between them. The woman must be freezing, the way she was so inadequately dressed. Her arms tightly bunched the paper-thin wrap around her quaking shoulders, but still she wanted to pretend that everything was all right and that she didn't need help.

'Come with me,' he said.

It was impulse that had him uttering the words, but once they were out he realised they made all kinds of sense. She was lost, all alone in Venice, and she was beautiful—even more beautiful than he'd first thought when she'd peeled off her mask. Her brandy-coloured eyes were large and cat-like in her high-cheekboned face, her painted curved lips like an invitation. He remembered the sight of her naked shoulder under the cloak, the cheap satin of the bodice cupping her breast, and a random thought amused him.

Sirena would hate her.

And wasn't that sufficient reason by itself?

Those cat-like eyes opened wide. *'Scusa?'*

'Come with me,' he said again. The seeds of a plan were already germinating—a plan that would benefit them both.

'You don't have to say that. You've already been too kind.'

'It's not about being kind. You would be doing me a favour.'

'How is that possible? We'd never met until a few moments ago. How can I possibly do you any favour?'

He held out his forearm to her, the leather of his sleeve creaking. 'Call it serendipity, if you prefer. Because I too have a costume ball to attend and I don't have a partner for the evening. So if you would do me the honour of accompanying me?'

She laughed a little, then shook her head. 'I've already told you—this is a costume. I wasn't waiting to be picked up.'

'I'm not trying to pick you up. I'm asking you to be my guest for the evening. But it is up to you, Rosa. Clearly you planned on going to a party tonight.'

He eased the mask from where she held it between the fingers clutching his cloak over her breasts and turned it slowly in his hands. She had no choice but to let it go. It was either let him take it or let go of the cloak.

'Why should you miss out on the biggest night of Carnevale,' he said, watching the way her eyes followed his hands as he thumbed the lace of her veil, 'just because you became separated from your friends?'

He could tell she was tempted—could all but taste her excitement at being handed a lifeline to an evening she'd all but given up on, even while questions and misgivings swirled in the depths of her eyes.

He smiled. He might have started this evening in a foul mood, and he knew that would have been reflected in his features, but he knew how to smile when it got him something he wanted. Knew how to turn on the charm when the need arose—whether he was involved in negotiations with an antagonistic foreign diplomat or romancing a woman he desired in his bed.

'Serendipity,' he repeated. 'A happy chance— for both of us. And the bonus is you'll get to wear my cloak a while longer.'

Her eyes lifted to meet his—long-lashed eyes, shy eyes, filled with uncertainty and nerves. Again, he was struck by her air of vulnerability. She was a very different animal from the women he usually met. An image of Sirena floated unbidden into his mind's eye—self-assured, self-centred Sirena, who wouldn't look vulnerable if she was alone in six feet of water and staring down a hungry shark. A very different animal indeed.

'It is very warm,' she said, 'thank you.'

'Is that a yes?'

She took a deep breath, her teeth troubling her bottom lip while a battle went on inside her, then gave a decisive nod, adding her own tentative smile in response. 'Why not?'

'Why not indeed?'

He didn't waste any time ushering her across the bridge and through the twisted *calles* towards the private entrance of the *palazzo* gardens, his mood considerably lighter than it had been earlier in the evening.

Because suddenly a night he hadn't been looking forward to had taken on an entirely different sheen. Not just because he was going to give Sirena a surprise and pay her back for the one she had orchestrated for him. But because he had a beautiful woman on his arm in one of the most beautiful cities in the world and the night was young.

And who knew where it would end?

CHAPTER THREE

ROSA'S HEART WAS tripping over itself as the gorgeous man placed her hand around the leather of his sleeve and cut a path through the crowds, and her feet struggled to keep up with his long strides.

Vittorio, he'd told her his name was, but that didn't make him any less a stranger. And he was leading her to a costume ball somewhere, or so he'd said. But she had no more detail than that. And she had nobody and nothing to blame for being here but a spark of impulse that had made her abandon every cautionary lesson she'd grown up with and provoked her into doing something so far out of her comfort zone she wondered if she'd ever find a way back.

'Why not?' she'd said in response to his invitation, in spite of the fact she could think of any number of reasons.

She'd never in her twenty-four years done anything as impetuous—or as reckless. Her brothers would no doubt add *stupid* to the description.

And yet, uncertainty and even stupidity aside, her night had turned another corner. One that had tiny bubbles of excitement fizzing in her blood.

Anticipation.

'It's not far,' he said, 'Are you still cold?'

'No.'

Quite the contrary. His cloak was like a shield against the weather, and his arm under hers felt solid and real. If anything, she was exhilarated, as though she'd embarked upon a mystery tour, or an adventure with an unknown destination. So many unknowns, and this man was at the top of the list.

She glanced up at him as he forged on with long strides through the narrow *calle*. He seemed eager to get where he was going now, almost as if he'd wasted too much time talking to her in the square and was making up for lost time. They passed a lamp that cast light and shadow on his profile, turning it into a moving feast of features—the strong lines of his jaw and nose, his high brow and dark eyes, and all surrounded by a thick mane of black hair.

'It's not far now,' he said, looking down at her.

For a moment—a second—his cobalt eyes met hers and snagged, and the bubbles in her blood spun and fizzed some more, and a warm glow stirred deep in her belly.

She stumbled and he caught her, not letting her fall, and the moment was gone, but even as she whispered her breathless thanks she resolved not to spend too much time staring into this man's eyes. At least not while she was walking.

'This way,' he said, steering her left down a narrow path away from the busy *calle*. Here, the ancient wall of a *palazzo* disappeared into the fog on one side, a high brick wall on the other, and with each step deeper along the dark path the sounds of the city behind became more and more muffled by the fog, until every cautionary tale she'd ever heard came back to mock her and the only sound she could hear was her own thudding heartbeat.

No, not the only sound, because their footsteps echoed in the narrow side alley and there also came the slap of water, the reflection of pale light on the shifting surface of the path ahead. But, no, that would mean—

And that was when she realised that the path ended in a dark recess with only the canal beyond.

A dead end.

Adrenaline spiked in her blood as anticipation morphed into fear. She'd come down this dark path willingly, with a man of whom she knew nothing apart from his name. If it even *was* his name.

'Vittorio,' she said, her steps dragging as she tried to pull her hand from where he had tucked it into his elbow. 'I think maybe I've changed my mind…'

'*Scusi?*'

He stopped and spun towards her, and in the

gloomy light his shadowed face and flashing eyes took on a frightening dimension. In this moment he could be a demon. A monster.

Her mouth went dry. She didn't want to stay to find out which. 'I should go home.'

She was struggling with the fastening of his cloak, even as she backed away, her fingers tangling with the clasp to free herself and give it back before she fled.

Already she could hear her brothers berating her, asking her why she'd agreed to go with someone she didn't know in the first place, telling her what a fool she'd been—and they'd be right. She would never live down the shame. She would regret for ever her one attempt at impetuosity.

'Rosa?'

A door swung open in the recess behind Vittorio, opening up to a fantasy world beyond. Lights twinkled in trees. A doorman looked to see who was outside and bowed his head when he spotted them waiting.

'Rosa?' Vittorio said again. 'We're here—at the *palazzo*.'

She blinked. Beyond the doorman there was a path between some trees and at the end of it a fountain, where water rose and fell to some unseen beat. 'At the ball?'

'Yes,' he said, and in the low light she could see the curve of his lips, as if he'd worked out why she'd suddenly felt the urge to flee. 'Or do you feel the need to remind me once again that you are just wearing a costume?'

Rosa had never been more grateful for the fog as she swallowed back a tide of embarrassment.

Dio, what must he think of me? First he finds me lost and helpless, and then I panic like I'm expecting him to attack me.

Chiara was right—she needed to toughen up. She wasn't in the village any more. She didn't have her father or her brothers to protect her. She needed to wise up and look after herself.

She attempted a smile in return. 'No. I'm so sorry—'

'No,' he said, offering her his arm again. '*I'm* sorry. Most people take a motorboat to the front entrance. I needed the exercise but walking made me late, so I was rushing. I should have warned you that we would be taking the side entrance.'

Her latest burst of adrenaline leeched out of her and she found an answering smile as she took his arm and let him lead her into a garden lit with tiny lights that magically turned a line of trees into carriages pulled by horses towards the *palazzo* beyond.

And as they entered this magical world she wondered… She'd been told to expect heavy security and bag searches at the ball, but this doorman had ushered them in without so much as blinking.

'What kind of ball is this?' she asked. 'Why are there no tickets and no bag searches?'

'A private function, by invitation only.'

She looked up at him. 'Are you sure it's all right for me to come, in that case?'

'I invited you, didn't I?'

They stopped just shy of the fountain, halfway across the garden by the soaring side wall of the *palazzo*, so she could take in the gardens and their magical lighting. To the left, a low wall topped with an ornate railing bordered the garden. The canal lay beyond, she guessed, though it was near impossible to make out anything through the fog, and the buildings opposite were no more than shifting apparitions in the mist.

The mist blurred the tops of the trees and turned the lights of those distant buildings into mere smudges, giving the garden a mystical air. To Rosa, it was almost as if Venice had shrunk to this one fairy-tale garden. The damp air was cold against her face, but she was deliciously warm under Vittorio's cloak and in no hurry to go inside. For inside there would be more guests—more strangers—and doubtless there would be friendships and connections between them and she would be the outsider. For now it was enough to deal with this one stranger.

More than enough when she thought about the way he looked at her—as if he was seeing inside her, reaching into a place where lurked her deepest fears and desires. For they both existed with this man. He seemed to scrape the surface of her nerve-endings away so everything she felt was raw. Primal. Exciting.

'What is this place?' she asked, watching the play of water spouting from the fat fish at the base of the three-tiered fountain. 'Who owns it?'

'It belongs to a friend of mine. Marcello's ancestors were *doges* of Venice and very rich. The *palazzo* dates back to the sixteenth century.'

'His family were rulers of Venice?'

'Some. Yes.'

'How do you even *know* someone like that?'

He paused, gave a shrug of his shoulders. 'My father and his go back a long way.'

'Why? Did your father work for him?'

He took a little time before he dipped his head to the side. 'Something like that.'

She nodded, understanding. 'I get that. My father services the mayor's cars in Zecce—the village in Puglia where I come from. He gets invited to the Christmas party every year. We used to get invited too, when we were children.'

'We?'

'My three older brothers and me. They're all married now, with their own families.'

She looked around at the gardens strung with lights and thought about the new nephew or niece who would be welcomed into the world in the next few weeks, and the money she'd wasted on her ticket for the ball tonight—money she could have used to pay for a visit home, along with a special gift for the new baby, and still have had change left over. She sighed at the waste.

'I paid one hundred euros for my ticket to the ball. That's one hundred euros down the drain.'

One eyebrow arched. 'That much?'

'I know. It's ridiculously expensive, and ours was one of the cheapest balls, so you're lucky to get invited to parties in a place like this for free. You can pay a lot more than I did, though. Hundreds more.'

She swallowed. She was babbling. She knew she was babbling. But something about this man's looming presence in the fog made her want to put more of herself into it and even up the score. He was so tall, so broad across the shoulders, his features so powerful. Everything about him spoke of power.

Because he hadn't said a word in the space she'd left, she felt compelled to continue. 'And then you have to have a costume, of course.'

'Of course.'

'Although I made my costume myself, I still had to buy the material.'

'Is that what you do, Rosa?' he asked as they resumed their walk towards the *palazzo*. 'Are you a designer?'

She laughed. 'Hardly. I'm not even a proper seamstress. I clean rooms at the Palazzo d'Velatte, a small hotel in the Dorsoduro *sestiere*. Do you know it?'

He shook his head.

'It's much smaller than this, but very grand.'

Steps led up to a pair of ancient wooden doors that swung open before them, as if whoever was inside had been anticipating their arrival.

She looked up at him. 'Do you ever get used to visiting your friend in such a grand place?'

He just smiled and said, 'Venice is quite special. It takes a little getting used to.'

Rosa looked up at the massive doors, at the light spilling from the interior, and took a deep breath. 'It's taking me a *lot* of getting used to.'

And then they entered the *palazzo*'s reception room and Rosa's eyes really popped. She'd thought the hotel where she worked was grand! Marketed as a one-time *palazzo*, and now a so-called boutique hotel, she'd thought it the epitome of style, capturing the faded elegance of times gone by.

It was true that the rooms were more spacious than she'd ever encountered, and the ceilings impossibly high—not to mention a pain to clean.

But the building seemed to have an air of neglect about it, as if it was sinking in on itself. The doors caught and snagged on the tiled floors, never quite fitting into the doorframes, and there were complaints from guests every other day that things didn't quite work right.

Elegant decay, she'd put it down to—until the day she'd taken out the rubbish to the waiting boat and witnessed a chunk of wall falling into the canal. She figured there was not much that was elegant about a wall crumbling piece by piece into the canal.

But here, in this place, she was confronted by a real *palazzo*—lavishly decorated from floor to soaring ceiling with rich frescoes and gilded reliefs, and impeccably furnished with what must be priceless antiques. From somewhere high above came the sounds of a string quartet, drifting down the spectacular staircase. And now she could see the hotel where she worked for what it really was. Faded…tired. A mere whisper of what it had been trying to emulate.

Another doorman stepped forward with a nod, and relieved Rosa of both Vittorio's leather cloak and her own wrap underneath.

'It's so beautiful,' she said, wide-eyed as she took it all in, rubbing her bare arms under the light of a Murano glass chandelier high above that was lit with at least one hundred globes.

'Are you cold?' he asked, watching her, his eyes raking over her, taking in her fitted bodice and the skirt with the weather-inappropriate hem.

'No.'

Not cold. Her goosebumps had nothing to do with the temperature. Rather, without her cloak and the gloom outside to keep her hidden from his gaze, she felt suddenly exposed. Crazy. She'd been so delighted with the way the design of the gown had turned out, so proud of her efforts after all the late nights she'd spent sewing, and she'd been eager to wear it tonight.

'You look so sexy,' Chiara had said, clapping her hands as Rosa performed a twirl for her. 'You'll have every man at the ball lining up to dance with you.'

She had *felt* sexy, and a little bit more wicked than she was used to—or at least she had felt that way then. But right now she had to resist the urge to tug up the bodice of her gown, where it hugged the curve of her breasts, and tug down the front of the skirt.

In a place such as this, where elegance and class oozed from the frescoes and antique glass chandeliers, bouncing light off myriad marble and gilded surfaces, she felt like a cheap bauble. Tacky. Like the fake glass trinkets that some of the shops passed off as Venetian glass when it had been made in some rip-off factory half a world away.

She wondered if Vittorio was suddenly regretting his rash impulse to invite her. Could he see how out of place she was?

Yes, she was supposed to be dressed as a courtesan, but she wished right now that she'd chosen a more expensive fabric or a subtler colour. Something with class that wasn't so brash and obvious. Something that contained at least a modicum of decency. Surely he had to see that she didn't belong here in the midst of all this luxury and opulence?

Except he wasn't looking at her with derision. Didn't look at her as if she was out of place. Instead she saw something else in his eyes. A spark. A flame. *Heat*.

And whatever it was low down in her belly that had flickered into life this night suddenly squeezed tight.

'You say you made your costume yourself?' he asked.

If she wasn't wrong, his voice had gone down an octave.

'Yes.'

'Very talented. There is just one thing missing.'

'What do you mean?'

But he already had his hands at her head. Her mask, she realised. She'd forgotten all about it.

And now he smoothed it down over her hair, adjusting the crown so that it was centred before straightening the lace of her veil over her eyes.

She didn't move a muscle to try to stop him and do it herself. She didn't want to stop him. Because all the while the gentle brush of his fingers against her skin and the smoothing of his hands on her hair set off a chain reaction of tingles under her scalp and skin, hypnotising her into inaction.

'There,' he said, removing his hands from her head. She had to stop herself from swaying after them. 'Perfection.'

'Vittorio!'

A masculine voice rang out from the top of the stairs, saving her from having to find a response when she had none.

'You're here!'

'Marcello!' Vittorio answered, his voice booming in the space. 'I promised you I'd be here, did I not?'

'With you,' the man said, jogging down the wide marble steps two by two, 'who can tell?'

He was dressed as a Harlequin, in colours of black and gold, and the leather of his shoes slapped on the marble stairs as he descended. He and Vittorio embraced—a man hug, a back-slap— before drawing apart.

'Vittorio,' the Harlequin said, 'it is good to see you.'

'And you,' Vittorio replied.

'And you've brought someone, I see,' he said, whipping off the mask over his eyes, his mouth curving into a smile as he held out one hand and bowed generously. 'Welcome, fair stranger. My name is Marcello Donato.'

The man was impossibly handsome. *Impossibly.* Olive-skinned, with dark eyes and brows, a sexy slash of a mouth and high cheekbones over which any number of supermodels would go to war with each other. But it was the warmth of his smile that made Rosa instinctively like the man.

'My name is Rosa.'

She took his hand and he drew her close and kissed both her cheeks.

'I'm right in thinking we've never met, aren't I?' he said as he released her. 'I'd be sure to remember if we had.'

'I've only just met Rosa myself,' Vittorio said, before she could answer. 'She lost her party in the fog. I thought it unfair that she missed out on the biggest night of Carnevale.'

Marcello nodded. 'That would be an injustice of massive proportions. Welcome, Rosa, I'm glad you found Vittorio.' He stepped back and regarded them critically. 'You make a good couple—the mad warrior protecting the runaway Princess.'

Vittorio snorted beside her.

'What's so funny?' she said.

'Marcello is known for his flights of fancy.'

'What can I say?' He beamed. 'I'm a romantic. Unlike this hard-hearted creature beside me, whom you managed to stumble upon.'

She filed the information away for future reference. The words had been said in jest, but she wondered if there wasn't an element of truth in them. 'So, tell me,' she said, 'what is this Princess hiding from?'

'That's easy,' he said. 'An evil serpent. But don't worry. Vittorio will protect you. There's not a serpent in the land that's a match for Vittorio.'

Something passed between the two men's eyes. A look. An understanding.

'What am I missing?' she asked, her eyes darting from one to the other.

'The fun,' Marcello said, pulling his mask back on. 'Everyone is upstairs on the second *piano nobile*. Come.'

Marcello was warm and welcoming, and nobody seemed to have any issues with the way she was dressed. Rosa began to relax. She'd been worrying about nothing.

Together they ascended the staircase to the *piano nobile*, where the principal reception rooms of the *palazzo* were housed one level above the waters of the canal. With its soaring ceilings, and rock crystal chandelier, Rosa could see that this level was even more breath-taking, more opulent, than the last. And the *pièce de résistance* was the impossibly ornate windows that spread generously across one wall.

'Is there a view?' she asked, tempted to look anyway. 'I mean, when it isn't foggy?'

'You'll have to come back,' Marcello said, ignoring the crowded reception rooms either side, filled with partygoers, and the music of Vivaldi coming from the string quartet, and walking to the windows before them. 'On a clear day you can see the Rialto Bridge to the right.'

Rosa peered through the fog, trying to make sense of the smudges of light. But if the Rialto Bridge was to the right... 'You're on the Grand Canal!'

Marcello shrugged and smiled. 'Not that you can tell today. But Venice wearing its shroud of fog is still a sight to behold, so enjoy. And now please excuse me while I find you some drinks.'

'We're in San Polo,' she said to Vittorio.

The hotel where she worked was in the Dorsoduro *sestiere*, the ball she was supposed to be attending was in the northern district of Cannaregio. Somehow she'd ended up lost between them and within a whisker of the sinuous Grand Canal, which would have hinted at her location if only she'd found it.

A smudge of light passed slowly by—a *va-*

poretto or a motorboat carefully navigating the fog-shrouded waterway—and Rosa's thoughts chugged with it. Vittorio had been kind, asking her to accompany him, but strictly speaking she wasn't lost any more.

She turned to him. 'I know where I am now.'

'Does that matter?'

'I mean, I'm not lost. At least, I can find my way home from here.'

He turned to her, putting his big hands on her shoulders as he looked down at her. 'Are you looking for yet another reason to escape?'

A wry smile kicked up one side of his mouth. He was laughing at her again, and she found she didn't mind—not when seeing his smile made her feel as if she was capturing something rare and true.

'I'm not—'

He cocked an eyebrow. 'Why are you so desperate to run away from me?'

He was wrong. She wasn't desperate to run away from him. Oh, sure, there'd been that moment when she'd panicked, at the end of the path outside the side gate, but she knew better now. Vittorio was no warrior or warlord, no demon or monster. He was a man, warm and real and powerful…a man who made her blood zing.

Except the warm weight of his hands on her shoulders and the probing questions in his eyes vanquished reasoned argument. There was only strength and heat and fear that it would be Vittorio who might change his mind. And then he'd take his hands away. And then she'd miss that contact and the heat and the zing and the pure exhilaration of being in his company.

A tiny worm of a thought squeezed its way through the connections in her brain. *Wasn't that reason enough to run?*

She was out of her depth with a man like him—a man who was clearly older and more worldly-wise, who moved in circles with people who owned entire *palazzos* and whose ancestors were amongst the *doges* of Venice. A man who made her feel stirrings in her belly, fizzing in her blood—things she wasn't used to feeling.

Nothing in the village—not a teenage crush on her maths teacher nor a dalliance with Antonio from the next village, who'd worked a few months in her father's workshop, had prepared her for meeting someone like Vittorio. She felt inadequate. Underdone.

She was dressed as a courtesan, a seductress, a temptress. But that was such a lie. She swallowed. She could hardly admit that, though.

'You invited me to this party tonight because I was lost and you felt sorry for me, because I was upset and was going to miss my own party.'

He snorted. 'I don't do things because I feel

sorry for people. I do things because I want to. I invited you to this party because I wanted to. And because I wanted you to be with me.' His hands squeezed her shoulders. 'So now, instead of trying to find all the reasons you shouldn't be here, how about you enjoy all the reasons you should?'

What could she say to that? 'In that case, it very much seems that I am stuck with you.'

'You are,' he said, with a smile that warmed her to her bones. 'At least for as long as this night lasts.'

'A toast.' Marcello said, arriving back with three glasses of Aperol spritz. He handed them each a glass. 'To Carnevale,' he said, raising his glass in a toast.

'To Carnevale,' said Rosa.

'To Carnevale,' echoed Vittorio, lifting his glass in Rosa's direction, 'And to the Venetian fog that delivered us Rosa.'

And if the words he uttered in his deep voice were not enough, the way Vittorio's piercing blue eyes looked at her above his glass made her blush all the way down to her toes. In that moment Rosa knew that this night would never last long enough, and that whatever else happened she would remember this night for ever.

She was skittish—so skittish. She was like a colt, untrained and unrehearsed, or a kitten, jumping at shadows and imaginary enemies. And it wasn't an act. He was good at spotting an ingénue, a pretender. He was used to women who played games and who made themselves out to be something they were not.

Just for a moment Vittorio wondered if he was doing the right thing, pitting her against Sirena. Maybe he should release her from her obvious unease and awkwardness and let her go back to her own world, if that was what she really wanted, back to what was, no doubt, the drudgery of her work and the worry of losing the paltry sum of one hundred euros.

Except Vittorio was selfish enough not to want to let her go.

He saw the way her eyes widened at every new discovery, at every exquisite Murano glass lamp, every frescoed wall or gilded mirror that stretched almost to the ceiling.

She was like a breath of fresh air in Vittorio's life. Unsophisticated and not pretending otherwise. She was a refreshing change when he had been feeling so jaded.

And she was a beautiful woman in a gown that fitted like a glove and make him ache to peel it off.

Why should he let her go?

CHAPTER FOUR

IT WASN'T A party or even a ball. It was like being part of a fairy-tale.

Rosa ascended the wide staircase to the second level above the water—yet another floor with soaring ceilings and exquisite antiques and furnishings. The music from the string quartet was louder here, richer, its sweet notes filling the gaps between the sound of laughter and high-spirited conversation coming from the party rooms either side of the staircase.

And the costumes! A brightly coloured peacock strutted by as they reached the top, all feathers and flashes of brilliant colour, and Rosa couldn't help but laugh in sheer wonderment as a couple with ice-white masks wearing elaborate gowns and suits of the deepest purple nodded regally as they strolled past arm in arm.

Rosa felt herself swept away into a different world of riches and costumes—a sumptuous world of fantasy—and only half wished that the man who had rescued her from the foggy *calles* wasn't quite so popular, because then she could keep him all to herself.

Everyone seemed to recognise Vittorio and to

want to throw out an exchange or a greeting. He was like a magnet to both men and women alike, but he always introduced her to them, including her in the conversation.

And, while her presence at his side wasn't questioned, she wondered what she might see if everyone wasn't wearing masks. Would the women's eyes be following Vittorio's every move because he was so compelling? Would they be looking at her in envy?

If she were in their place she would.

And suddenly the music and the costumes and the amazing sumptuousness of the *palazzo* bled into a heady mix that made her head spin. She was part of a Venice she'd never seen and had only ever imagined.

Suddenly there was a shriek of delight from the other wing, and a commotion as someone made their way through the crowds into the room.

'Vittorio!' a woman cried, bursting through the partygoers. 'I just heard you were here. Where have you been hiding all this time?'

But not just any woman.

Cleopatra.

Her sleek black bob was adorned with golden beads, the circlet at her forehead topped with an asp. Like Vittorio, she hadn't bothered with a mask. Her eyes were kohled, their lids painted turquoise-blue, and her dress was simply amazing.

Cut low—*really* low—over the smooth globes of her breasts, it was constructed entirely of beads in gold and bronze and silver, its short skirt just strings of the shiny beads that shifted and flashed skin with her every movement.

It wasn't so much a dress, Rosa thought as she took a step back to make room for the woman to reach up and kiss Vittorio on both cheeks, as an invitation. It showed the wearer's body off to perfection.

Cleopatra left her face close to his. 'Everyone has been waiting hours for you,' she chided, before she stood back to take in what he was wearing.

Or maybe to give him another chance to see her spectacular costume.

She held her hands out wide. 'But must you always look so dramatic? It's supposed to be a costume party.'

'I'm wearing a costume.'

'If you say so—but can't you for once dress out of character?'

'Sirena,' he said, ignoring her question as he reached for Rosa's hand, pulling her back into his orbit. 'I'd like you to meet a friend of mine. Rosa, this is Sirena, the daughter of one of my father's oldest friends.'

'Oh,' she said, with a knowing laugh, 'I'm *far* more than that.'

And then, for the first time, Sirena seemed to notice that there was someone standing next to Vittorio. She turned her head and looked Rosa up and down, letting her eyes tell Rosa what she thought about his 'friend'.

'Ciao,' she said, her voice deadpan, and Rosa couldn't be certain that she was saying hello as opposed to giving her a dismissal.

She immediately turned back to Vittorio, angling her back towards Rosa.

Definitely a dismissal.

'Vittorio, come with me—all our friends are in the other room.'

'I'm here with Rosa.'

'With who? Oh…'

She gave Rosa another look up and down, her eyes evaluating her as if she was a rival for Vittorio's affections. Ridiculous. She'd only just met the man tonight. But she wasn't mistaken. There was clear animosity in the woman's eyes.

'And what do you think of Vittorio's outfit…? What was your name again?'

'Rosa,' Vittorio growled. 'Her name is Rosa. It's not that difficult.'

'Of course it's not.' Sirena gave a lilting laugh as she turned to the woman whose name she couldn't remember and smiled. 'What do you think of Vittorio's outfit? Don't you think it's a bit over the top?'

'I like it,' she said. 'I like the blue of the leather. It matches his eyes.'

'It's not just blue, though, is it?' Sirena said dismissively. 'It's more like *royal* blue—isn't it, Vittorio?'

'That's enough, Sirena.'

'Well, I would have said it was *royal* blue.'

'Enough, I said.'

The woman pouted and stretched herself cat-like along the brocade chaise longue behind her, the beads of her skirt falling in a liquid slide to reveal the tops of her long, slender legs—legs that ended in sandals with straps that wound their way enticingly around her ankles.

The woman made an exquisite Cleopatra. But then, she was so exquisitely beautiful the real Cleopatra would no doubt have wanted to scratch out her eyes.

'It's all right, Vittorio, despite our difference in opinion Rosa and I are going to be good friends.' She smiled regally at Rosa. 'I like *your* costume,' she said.

For the space of one millisecond Rosa thought the woman was warming to her, wanted so much to believe she meant what she'd said. Rosa had spent many midnight hours perched over her mother's old sewing machine, battling with the slippery material and trying to get the seams and the fit just right. But then she saw the snigger barely contained beneath the smile and realised the woman hadn't been handing out a compliment.

'Rosa made it herself—didn't you, Rosa?'

'I did.'

Cleopatra's perfectly threaded eyebrows shot up. 'How...*enterprising.*'

Vittorio's presence beside her lent Rosa a strength she hadn't known she had, reminding her of what her brothers had always told her—not to be cowed by bullies but to stand up to them.

Her brothers were right, but it was a lot easier to take their advice when she had a man like Vittorio standing beside her.

Rosa simply smiled, not wanting to show what she really thought. 'Thank you. Your costume is lovely too. Did you make it yourself?'

The other woman stared at her as if she had three heads. 'Of course I didn't make it myself.'

'A shame,' Rosa said. 'If you had you might have noticed that there's a loose thread...'

She reached a hand out to the imaginary thread and the woman bolted upright and onto her sandalled feet, a whole lot less elegantly than she had reclined, no doubt imagining one tug of Rosa's hand unleashing a waterfall of glass beads across the Persian carpet.

'This gown is an Emilio Ferraro creation. Of *course* there's no loose thread.'

'Oh, I'm sorry. I must have been mistaken.'

Sirena sniffed, jerked her eyes from Rosa's and placed a possessive hand on Vittorio's chest. 'Come and see our friends when you're free. You won't *believe* what they're wearing. I'll be waiting for you.'

And with a swish of her beaded hair and skirt she was gone.

'That,' said Vittorio, 'was Sirena.'

'Cyclone Sirena, you mean,' Rosa said, watching the woman spinning out of the room as quickly as she'd come in, leaving a trail of devastation in her wake.

She heard a snort and looked up to see Vittorio smiling down at her. It was a real smile that warmed her bone-deep, so different from one of Sirena's ice-cold glares.

'You handled that very well.'

'And you thought I wouldn't?' she said. 'My brothers taught me to stand up to bullies.' She didn't mention that it was Vittorio's presence that had given her the courage to heed her brothers' advice.

'Good advice,' he said, nodding. 'If she finds that thread you saw she'll bust the balls of her precious Emilio.'

Rosa returned his smile with one of her own. 'There was no thread.'

And Vittorio laughed—a rich bellow that was

laced with approval and that made a tide of happiness well up inside her.

'Thank you,' he said, his arm going around her shoulders as he leaned down to kiss her cheek. 'For the best belly laugh I've had in a long time.'

It wasn't really a kiss. Mouth to cheek…a brush of a whiskered jaw…a momentary meeting of lips and skin—probably the same kind of kiss he might bestow upon a great-aunt. Even his arm was gone from her shoulder in an instant. Yet to Rosa it felt far more momentous.

It was the single most exciting moment in her life since she'd arrived in Venice.

Chiara had told her that magical things could happen at Carnevale. She'd told her a whole lot of things and Rosa hadn't believed her. She'd suspected it was just part of Chiara's sales technique, in order to persuade Rosa to part with so much money and go along to the ball with her.

But maybe her friend had been right. Rosa had been kissed by a man. She couldn't wait to tell her friend.

'You're blushing,' said Vittorio, his head at an angle as he looked down at her.

She felt her blush deepen and dropped her head. 'Yes, it's silly, I know.'

He put his hand to her chin and lifted her face to his. 'No,' he said. 'It's delightful. It's been a long time since I saw a woman blush.'

She blinked up at him, her skin tingling where his fingers lingered.

Oh, boy.

Talk about a distraction… She'd wanted to ask him more about Sirena, but the woman had faded into insignificance. Now all she could think about was Vittorio and the way he made her feel.

'Come, come!' said Marcello, clapping his hands as he walked into the room to gather everyone. 'The entertainment downstairs is about to begin. You don't want to miss it.'

Downstairs, the entire level of the *piano nobile* had been divided into performance areas, with stages and dramatic velvet drapes, and they spent the next hour wandering between the rooms to see the spectacle of gymnasts and jugglers and opera singers, and aerobatic performers who spun on ropes in the air. Then it was the turn of the clowns, and Rosa was soon almost doubled up with laughter at their antics.

She found herself thinking about Chiara and wondering how her night was going. They'd treated themselves to the cheapest tickets to the cheapest Carnevale ball they could find—and that only gave admission to the dancing segment of the evening. They hadn't been able to afford the price for the dinner and entertainment that came first. But surely even that entertainment would be no match for this.

And then Vittorio took her hand in his and she stopped thinking about Chiara, because her heart gave a little lurch that switched off her brain.

She looked sideways up at him to find him watching her, the cobalt of his eyes a shade deeper, his sensual slash of mouth curled up at the ends.

He gave the slightest squeeze of her hand before he let her go, and she turned her eyes back to the entertainment. But suddenly she wasn't laughing any more. Her chest felt too tight, her blood was buzzing, and she was imagining all kinds of impossible things.

Unimaginable things.

Chiara had said that magical things could happen at Carnevale.

Rosa had been a fool not to believe her.

She could *feel* the magic. It was in the air all around her. It was in the gilded frames and lush silks and crystal chandeliers. It was in the exquisite *trompe l'oeils* that adorned the walls with views of gardens that had only ever existed in the artist's eyes. And magic was pulsing alongside her, in leather of blue and gold, in a man with a presence she couldn't ignore—a man who had the ability to shake the very foundations of her world with just one look from his cobalt blue eyes.

Chiara had said she might meet the man of her dreams tonight. A man who had the power to tempt her to give up her most cherished possession.

She hadn't believed that either.

It would have to be a special kind of man for her to want to take such a momentous step. A *very* special kind of man.

Vittorio?

Her heart squeezed so tightly that she had to suck in a breath to ease the constriction.

Impossible. Life didn't work that way.

But what if Chiara had been right?

And what if Vittorio was the one?

She glanced up to sneak another look at him and found him already gazing down at her, his midnight hair framing the quizzical expression on his strong face.

His heart-stoppingly beautiful, strong face.

And she thought it would be madness not to find out.

Sirena either had spies everywhere, or she had a knack for knowing when Rosa had left his side for five minutes. The entertainment was finished but, while the party wouldn't wind down until dawn, Vittorio had other plans. Plans that didn't include Sirena, no matter how hard she tried to join in.

'This is supposed to be a *party*,' Sirena sulked conspiratorially to Marcello when she cornered him standing at the top of the stairs, where Vittorio was waiting for Rosa so they could say their goodbyes. 'A party for *friends*. An *exclusive* party. But did you see that woman Vittorio dragged along?'

'Her name is Rosa.'

Sirena took no notice. 'Did you see what she was wearing, Marcello? It was appalling.'

'Nobody's listening, Sirena,' Vittorio said dismissively.

'Rosa seems very nice,' said Marcello. 'And I like her costume.'

Vittorio nodded. 'She *is* nice. *Very* nice.' He thought about the way she'd pulled that ruse with the loose thread and smiled. 'Clever, too.'

Sirena pouted, her hand on Marcello's arm, pleading. 'She wasn't even invited.'

'*I* invited her.'

'You know what I mean. Someone like her wouldn't normally be allowed anywhere near here.'

'Sirena, give it up.' Vittorio turned away, searching for Rosa. The sooner he got her away from here—away from Sirena—the better.

'That's our Vittorio for you,' Marcello said, trying to hose down the antagonism between his guests, playing his life-long role of peacemaker to perfection. 'Always bringing home the strays. Birds fallen from their nests. Abandoned puppies. It made no difference. Vittorio, do you remember that bag of kittens we found snagged on the side of the river that day? *Dio*, how long ago was that? Twenty years?'

Vittorio grunted, hoping that Rosa was nowhere within earshot, because he didn't want her overhearing any of this.

He did remember that day. Marcello had been visiting. They'd wandered far and wide beyond the castle walls that day—much further than Vittorio had been permitted to roam. They'd both been about ten years old, and filled with the curiosity and compulsion of young boys to explore their world.

They'd been wading in the stream, chasing the silvery flashes of fish in the shallows, when they'd heard the pitiful cries. By the time they'd found the bag and pulled it from the stream all but one of the kittens had perished, and the plaintive mewls of the lone survivor had been heartrending. Vittorio had tucked the tiny shivering creature into his shirt and hurried back to the castle.

'So now you're saving sweet young things who get themselves lost in the streets of Venice? Quite the hero you've turned out to be,' said Sirena.

'It's lucky Vittorio was in the right place at the right time,' Marcello said, still doing his utmost to pour oil on troubled waters. 'Rosa would have had a dreary night by herself otherwise.'

Sirena bristled, ignoring Marcello's peacekeeping efforts. 'And does your father know you've found another stray?'

Vittorio sighed. *Where the hell was Rosa?* 'What's who I bring to a party got to do with my father?'

'Only that the three of us might finally settle our differences and work out a timeline for uniting our two families. That's what was supposed to happen tonight. That's what was intended.'

'Intended by whom? By your father and mine? By you? Because it certainly wasn't intended by me—tonight or any other night.'

He turned away. Where *was* she?

'Oh, Vittorio…' he heard Sirena say behind his back, and he recognised the change in her voice as she switched on the charm offensive. He heard the slither of beads and when he turned back he saw that she'd dropped Marcello's arm and edged herself closer to him. She placed one hand on his chest and snaked it around his neck. 'Do you *have* to play so hard to get? You know we're made for each other. And while I admit it's been fun at times, playing this game of cat and mouse, it gets so tiring…always keeping up the charade.'

Vittorio put his hand over her forearm and sighed. 'You're right, Sirena. It *is* tiring,' he said. 'I think it has gone on long enough.'

'You see?' she said, her smile widening. 'I knew you'd think it was time we worked this ou

We have to start making plans. Marcello will be your best man, surely?'

She didn't let her eyes shift from her target as Marcello, knowing it should be the groom who asked him, muttered an anxious, 'I'd be honoured, of course.'

'We'll have to have the wedding in the cathedral in Andachstein, of course,' Sirena said, as if Marcello hadn't uttered a word, 'and in spring. It's so beautiful in Andachstein in spring. But where should we honeymoon? We *have* to start planning, Vittorio. It's so exciting.'

Her nails were raking the skin at the back of his neck, but if the woman thought she was stroking his senses into compliance she was very much mistaken.

He put his hand over her forearm, pulling her hand away before he dropped it unceremoniously into what little space there was between them.

'No, Sirena. What I meant was that this farce has gone on long enough. Can you for once accept that whatever our fathers might have schemed, whatever they promised you, and whatever fantasy you've been nurturing in your mind, it's never going to happen. That is my promise to you.'

'But Vittorio,' she said, once again reaching out for him, with a note of hysteria in her voice this time. 'You can't be serious. You can't mean that.'

'How many times do I have to tell you before you accept the truth?'

'The truth is you're a playboy—everyone knows that. But you have to settle down some time.'

'Maybe I do,' he conceded, and it was the only concession he was prepared to make. 'But when I settle down it won't be with you.'

She spun away in a clatter of beads. 'You bastard!' She turned her regal chin over one shoulder and glared at him, the rage in her eyes all hellfire and ice. 'Go back and slum it with your little village slut, then. See if I care.'

Finally the real Sirena had emerged. He sighed. What kind of man would want to hitch himself to *that*, no matter the packaging? 'What you care or don't care about is not my concern, Sirena. But, for the record, that's exactly what I plan to do.'

Watching Sirena storm off, her sandalled feet slapping hard on the marble floor, was one of the most satisfying yet exhausting moments of Vittorio's life. Maybe she had finally got it through her head that there was never going to be a marriage between them. *Dio*, he was sick of this world of arranged marriages and false emotions.

But right now he had more pressing needs. He needed to find Rosa. He'd been wrong to bring her here. He'd exposed her to the best and the worst aspects of his life. And he'd exposed her to the worst of himself, using her as cannon fodder to make a point to a woman he had no intention of marrying.

What had he been thinking, inviting her here tonight? She deserved to be treated better than the way he had treated her. She'd been out of her depth—he'd known that from the start. She'd been overawed by the wealth and sumptuousness of this world she'd been given a glimpse of and yet she had handled herself supremely well, dealing with Sirena's antagonism with a courage he hadn't anticipated.

He slapped Marcello on the back in acknowledgement of what he'd attempted and told him he'd be back soon.

He didn't want to contemplate the carnage if Sirena found Rosa before he did. He'd never forgive himself. He was already feeling ill at ease for taking advantage of Rosa's circumstances the way he had. Serendipity, he'd called it. *Serendipity nothing*. He'd been out-and-out opportunistic. He'd charged Sirena with that same crime, and yet he was guilty of the charge himself. When he'd found Rosa he'd seen a decoy—a buffer for Sirena's insistent attention.

He should just take Rosa home, back to her dingy hotel and her humdrum life. Maybe she would be relieved to be back in her own world. Maybe she would see it as an escape. She should.

He wandered from room to room, brushing aside the calls to him to stop and talk.

He knew he should take her home. Except part of him didn't want to let her go—not just yet. His final words to Sirena hadn't been all bluff. Not when he thought about Rosa's upturned face looking into his. He remembered the change in her expression, her laughter drying up, her lips slightly parted. He remembered the hitch in her breath and the sudden rise of her chest.

He'd seen the way she'd gazed up into his eyes.

Rosa had been the best part of his evening.

He hated it that it had to end. And he had enough experience of the female to know that she didn't want it to end just yet either.

Eventually he found Rosa, surrounded by a group of guests he recognised—members of Sirena's retinue, simpering men and women who were her 'rent-a-court', always sitting around waiting on her every word, waiting for a rare treat to be dispensed. Now they were formed around Rosa like some kind of Praetorian Guard, looking at Rosa as if *she* was the treat.

Sirena's work, no doubt. It had her fingerprints all over it.

'Here you are,' he said, barely able to keep the snarl from his voice as he surveyed the smug-looking group. 'I've been looking everywhere for you.'

She didn't look pleased to see him. Her eyes didn't meet his with relief, or with the delight he would have preferred. The brandy in her eyes was un-warmed. Non-committal. Even her body language had changed, her movements stiff and formal.

'I've been making some new friends,' she said.

He glanced around at the six of them, all dressed the same—or rather, *un*dressed the same. The men were bare-chested, wearing white kilts, blue and white striped headdresses and wide gold armbands. The women had the addition of a golden bralette.

Cleopatra's so-called friends. More like a guard of honour. And he knew that, like Sirena, they were capable of tearing an unsuspecting person to pieces. He wasn't the only one who would be able to see her lack of sophistication and absence of guile. Rosa was like the first bright flare of a matchstick in a darkened room. She was all vulnerability in a world of weary cynicism.

'I'm sorry to disappoint your new *friends*,' he lied, eyeballing each and every one of their heavily kohled eyes, 'but we're leaving. I'm taking you home.'

Rosa's chin kicked up. 'What if I'm not ready to go home? I know where I am now. I can find my own way.'

'We can take you,' one of her new friends offered, with a lean and hungry smile.

'Yes,' said another, his lips drawing hyena-like over his teeth as he took one of her hands. 'Stay a little longer, Rosa. We'll see that you get home.'

'It's up to you,' Vittorio told her.

There was no hiding the growl in his voice even as he had to force himself to back off—because if she didn't want him he could hardly drag her out of here, no matter that his inner caveman was insisting he simply throw her over his shoulder and leave. She was a grown-up, with a mind of her own, and if she was foolish enough to choose them over her it would be on her own head.

But still the idea sat uneasily with him.

She looked from the group to Vittorio and he saw the indecision in her eyes, the brittle wall of resistance she'd erected around herself waver. And, like that moment by the bridge, when he'd seen her shoulders slump as she recognised the hopelessness of her situation, he could tell the moment she made a decision.

'No,' she said to the group with a smile of apology. 'Thank you for your kind offer. But it's late and I have to work tomorrow.'

Vittorio grunted his approval while they pleaded with her to reconsider. So she'd witnessed what was in their eyes and decided he was the lesser of two evils? At least she had *that* much sense.

But it occurred to him that he might have to rethink his plans for the evening. Things had changed in the balance between them. He'd thought she was learning to trust him, losing her skittishness, but something had happened in the time she'd been out of his sight. Something that had fractured the tentative bond that had been developing between them.

It was too bad, but it was hardly the end of the world.

Tomorrow he would return to Andachstein, a tiny coastal principality nestled between Italy and Slovenia. He had duties there. There was a film festival gala to attend and a new hospital wing to be opened, along with school visits to make—all part of his royal duties as heir. So he'd see Rosa safely home now, and then he'd head back to the family *palazzo*—the legacy of a match between the daughter of a Venetian aristocrat and one of Andachstein's ancestral princes.

No doubt his father would be waiting for the news he'd been wanting to hear for years. He was not going to be happy to hear there was none.

'I'll be fine now,' she said, once they were out of the room. 'I'll find my own way home.'

'I don't think so.'

'Listen, Vittorio—'

'No. *You* listen. If you think I'm going to let you loose in the fog-bound *calles* at this time of the morning, after half the city's been partying all night, you've got another think coming. That lot upstairs aren't the only ones who'd take advantage of a lone woman feeling her way home in the fog.'

She swallowed, and he saw the kick of her throat even as her eyes flashed defiantly. He could tell she saw the sense in his words, even if she didn't want to.

'So I'm still stuck with you, then,' she said.

'So it would seem.'

She turned her head away in resignation and they descended the staircase in silence, together but apart, the earlier warmth they'd shared having dissipated.

His mood blackened with every step, returning him to that dark place he'd been earlier in the evening. It didn't help that Rosa had lost the air of wonderment she'd arrived with. It didn't help that she couldn't find him a smile and that he had been relegated to mere chaperone—one that she was only putting up with under sufferance. It raised his hackles.

'I'm sorry,' he said, maybe a little more brusquely than he'd have preferred, but then, he wasn't in the mood for pleasantries. 'Perhaps I shouldn't have brought you here. I shouldn't have invited you.'

'Why shouldn't you have invited me?' she asked. 'Because I don't belong? Because I'm no better than a little village slut for you to slum it with?'

'You heard. How much did you hear?'

'I heard enough.'

Vittorio wanted to slam his head against the nearest wall. As if it wasn't enough that Sirena had subjected her to those poisoned barbs face to face, Rosa had heard what Sirena had said behind her back.

'I didn't call you that.'

'I didn't hear you deny it,' she said, but she didn't sound angry, as she had every right to. She sounded...disappointed.

He could have explained that there would have been no point, that it wasn't what *he* thought of her and that Sirena would have taken no notice, but she was right. He hadn't made any attempt to deny or correct it.

Dio. What a mess.

They collected their cloaks in silence, and only three words were playing over and over in Rosa's mind.

Little village slut.

Stone-faced, Vittorio covered her shoulders

with first her own cloak and then his cursed scented leather cloak. She hated the fact that it smelt so good now, and tried to slip away from beneath it.

'I don't need that.'

But he persisted, like a father whose patience with his recalcitrant toddler was all but used up. 'Yes, you do,' he insisted, and he turned her towards him and did up the fancy clasp she'd had trouble undoing before.

She looked everywhere but at him. And the moment he released her she turned away from his touch and his stony features, wishing she could so easily turn away from the warmth of his cloak and the promise it had given her.

Instead, the evening had finished up a huge disappointment. It had been a rollercoaster of emotions from the start, from excitement to panic to despair to hope. Or a kind of hope. But now she could see that that hope had been like those strings of beads in the glamorous Sirena's skirt, and that one pulled thread would have seen it fall apart and skitter away into a million irreconcilable parts.

And now there was just the end to be negotiated.

She took a deep breath. She'd had a night out. A fantasy night such as she could never have expected or afforded. She'd had an experience with which to reassure Chiara, when her friend apologised profusely about losing her in the crowds without her phone or ticket, as she expected she would.

And she'd had a glimmer of something special. Of a man who looked like a warrior, a man who'd been chivalrous and generous enough to include her in his world, a man who simultaneously excited and frightened her, a man who made her insides curl when he looked at her as if she was something special.

At least she imagined that was what he'd been thinking.

She sighed. Soon she would be back home in the tiny basement apartment she shared with Chiara and this night would be just a memory.

Little village slut.

The words kept on circling in Rosa's mind. It was true, she did come from a small village in the heel of Italy. A dot of a town, to be sure. But that was where the truth ended. And it was so unfair.

'They're only words,' her brothers had told her when she'd been bullied at school. *'Words can't wound you.'*

She'd wanted to believe her brothers. Maybe she had for a time—except perhaps now, because the man she'd thought he was, the man she'd built up in her mind, had turned out to be somebody else. The man who had been a stranger to her, the man she'd thought was something else entirely, was a stranger still.

'Where are we going?' she asked, when Vittorio led her down the steps into the garden.

'We're going home by motorboat,' he said, as he steered her to the big wooden doors that were opened for them onto the Grand Canal.

Rosa shivered as the damp air surged in. She'd forgotten how very cold the fog was—although that didn't make her want to be any more grateful for Vittorio's cloak or want to tell him that he'd been right. She wouldn't give him the satisfaction.

A few steps below them a motorboat sat rocking on the lapping waters of the canal. Fog still clung low, swirling in the air and rendering the glow of lights to ghostly smudges.

'Palazzo D'Marburg,' he told the driver, handing her into the boat before bundling her into the covered interior.

The motor chugged into life once they were seated, and the boat pulled away slowly into the canal, still moving slowly when it cleared the dock. It was so painfully slow that Rosa wished they had walked after all. The journey home would take for ever at this rate, and the interior of the cabin was already too small for the both of them. Too intimate. Vittorio took up too much of the space and sucked up the remaining oxygen in the cabin. Was it any wonder she was breathless?

And meanwhile the man opposite her had turned to stone, his expression grim, his body language saying he was a man whose patience had worn thin and who was stoically waiting to be rid of her. Or a man who was sulking because she wasn't falling victim to his charms any more.

Well, she was waiting too—to be free of this warrior whose charms had long since expired.

Maybe she should have stayed at the party. She'd been meeting people and having fun, hadn't she? Okay, so she hadn't liked the way a couple of them had looked at her enough to want them to take her home, but at least she'd been able to breathe there, and her heart hadn't tripped over itself like it did every time this man so much as looked at her.

She would have been perfectly all right if she'd stayed. And Marcello would have looked after her if he'd thought she was in any danger. Vittorio was such a drama queen.

He chose that moment to shift in his seat, his big knee brushing against her leg, and she bristled in response. What *was* it about the man? He couldn't move without making her notice. He took up so much space. He had such presence. He made her feel small. Insignificant.

She sucked in air and, and as if it wasn't bad enough that she had to put up with the scent of him, even the air now tasted of him.

Suddenly it was all too much—the fog and the rocking and the cursed muffled silence. It was like being entombed with one of those Chinese stone warriors from the Terracotta Army she'd seen on display at a museum in Rome on a school visit. And she wasn't ready to be entombed.

She launched herself at the door that led to the small rear deck.

'It's too cold out there,' he growled.

'I don't care!' she flung back at him, shoving her way through the door.

She had no choice. She had to get outside. She had to escape.

The cold air hit her skin like a slap in the face, but at least the air outside didn't taste of Vittorio and smell like Vittorio, and it wasn't filled with the bulk of him. Finally she could breathe again. She gulped in great lungsful of it, letting it cleanse her senses even as she huddled her arms around her chest.

Of course he followed her, as she'd known he would, standing beside her silently like a sentinel. She didn't have to turn her head to know he was there. She could sense his presence. Feel his heat. Cursed man.

The motorboat chugged and rocked its way slowly along the canal. It was other-worldly. The sounds and sights of the city had vanished. Items appeared suddenly out of the fog—a lamp on a post, another motorboat edging its way cautiously by—and then just as quickly were swallowed up again.

And he was the most other worldly part of it all.

A fantasy gone wrong.

She searched through the fog, suddenly frantic, trying to find a reference point so that she could tell how long this trip would last. But there was nothing. Not a hint of where they were. No clue to how long she would be forced to endure this torture.

Nothing but silence. Tension. And her utter disappointment with how this evening had ended when it had started out with such excitement. Such promise.

Like a rubber band stretched too far, she snapped. 'Why did you ask me to come with you tonight?'

Slowly, almost as slowly as the boat they were travelling on, he turned his head towards her. His expression told her nothing and his face was a mask of stone.

'Because you were lost and alone. Because I thought I could help.'

She scoffed. 'I think we both know that's not true, Vittorio. I don't want that line you spun me about chivalry and concern for my happiness and well-being and not wanting me to miss out on the last night of Carnevale. I want the real reason.'

He was silent for a few seconds, but Rosa wasn't going to give him time to make something else up.

She gathered the strength to ask the question that had been plaguing her ever since that woman dressed as Cleopatra had burst onto the scene. 'Who is Sirena to you?' she demanded. 'What claim does she hold over you?'

'None. Sirena is nothing to me.'

Rosa gave a very unladylike snort, and if it made her sound like the country girl she was, instead of some pampered city girl with polished manners, she didn't give a damn. 'You expect me to believe that when I witnessed her draped all over you like a limpet.'

'That meant nothing,' he said. 'Whatever Sirena likes to think.'

She shook her head. 'She thinks you're going to marry her!'

He looked shocked.

'I was there,' she said. 'I heard what she said.'

He took a deep breath and sighed, long and hard. 'My father wants me married. It would suit him if I married his friend's daughter. That is all.'

'That's *all*?' She laughed into the mist, her breath turning to fog. 'What I don't understand is why I had to get dragged into your mess. Did you know she'd be at the ball tonight?'

'I'd had word.'

Finally something that made sense. She gave a long sigh of her own. 'So there we have it,' she said, nodding her head as she looked out into the mist and the pieces of the puzzle fell into place. 'You invited me to come with you to make her jealous.'

'No! It was never to make her jealous.'

'Then what? To run interference? To make a point? Was it sport you had in mind? Is *that* what asking me to go with you was all about?'

He said nothing—which told her everything she needed to know.

She heard his deep breath in, felt him shift as he ran his hand through his untamed hair.

'You were lost.'

'One of your strays?'

He sniffed. 'Maybe. And I thought I could help you—and you could help me—at the same time.'

She shook her head 'Bottom line, Vittorio, you used me.' Even as she said the words tiny tears squeezed from her eyes. She'd had such high hopes for this night. He'd made her think all kinds of things. That she mattered. That he cared. That she wanted…

'Rosa…'

'No,' she said, turning further away, because he didn't care, and the disappointment of the evening was weighing heavily down on her, crushing her.

'Rosa.' His hands were on her shoulders. 'I'm sorry.'

'And that's supposed to make it better? That's supposed to make it all right?'

She hated it that her voice sounded so quaky, that she sounded so needy, when she'd thought that growing up with three brothers had toughened her up for anything. She hated it that she could feel the warm puff of his breath on her hair. She hated it that his hands were on her shoulders and it wasn't enough. She hated herself because she wanted more.

'No, it's not all right. I hurt you.'

She sniffed as he turned her with his big hands, but she didn't resist. Didn't resist when he drew her against his body and wrapped his arms around her. Didn't object when she felt him dip his head and kiss her hair.

'Can you forgive me?'

It felt so warm, being cradled against his big body. So firm. So hard. And the drumbeat of his heart added another note to the lullaby chugging of the engine, made the movement of the boat beneath their feet like the rocking of a cradle.

'I'm sorry that I hurt you,' he said. 'I knew Sirena would be angry. The only reason I said I should never have invited you was because I'd anticipated Sirena's reaction. I knew she'd be furious and she didn't disappoint. To subject you to that was unthinkable. You didn't deserve that.'

She should pull away. Her tears had passed and she should put distance between them, she knew. He'd treated her shamefully and she should want nothing more to do with him, apology or no. Why should she forgive him?

But she remembered the way he'd looked at her during the entertainment. She remembered the warmth of his hand, that shared moment when it had seemed the world was made of magic. His body felt so good next to hers. So very warm. And that was a kind of magic too. Was it wrong to want the magic to last just a little bit longer?

He stroked her back and she felt the crushing disappointment of the evening ebb slowly away. 'It was a good party,' she said. It was a concession of sorts. Because it *had* been an experience. She had so much to tell Chiara in the morning. 'I enjoyed it. Most of it.'

He squeezed his arms and she felt the press of his lips to her hair again, and she knew she wasn't drawing away from him any time soon.

'That's good. I'm sorry that Sirena had to spoil it for you.' A moment later he added, 'No, I'm sorry *I* had to spoil it for you.'

Rosa thought about how the woman had looked in her costume, her limbs so long, her skin so smooth and perfect. The woman had made Rosa feel so ordinary. So drab and inconsequential. The woman would have made the real Cleopatra feel inconsequential.

'She's very beautiful, isn't she?'

He sighed and placed his chin on her head. 'Beauty is an empty vessel,' he said, his deep voice a bare whisper over the chug of the motor. 'It needs something to fill it. Something meaningful and worthwhile to flesh it out and make it whole.'

She was struck by his whispered words. 'Where did you hear that?'

'Something my mother once said.'

'She sounds very wise.'

'She could be, at times.' A pause. A sigh. 'She's dead now.'

'I'm sorry.'

'Thank you, but it's not your fault.'

'I understand. But my mother is gone too. She was diagnosed with leukaemia. She died three years ago. There's not a day goes by that I don't think about her...that I don't miss her.'

He shook his head. 'And now it's my turn to say I'm sorry, and your turn to say it's not my fault.'

She laughed a little at his words, then stopped. The sound was so unexpected when her thoughts had been tuned to disappointment. 'The language of death. It's so complicated.'

He loosened one arm and lifted his hand to her

face, touching her gently with the knuckle of one finger. He was so gentle that she barely felt the brush of his skin against hers, and yet his touch sent bone-deep tremors through her. Made her want to lean into his hand.

Then he took her chin and lifted her face to his. 'Maybe instead we should talk the language of the living.'

Her breath hitched in her throat. His hand was warm against her skin, his face filling her vision. She swallowed. 'I think I'd prefer that.'

His eyes were dark blue against the foggy night and the force of them pulled her towards him.

Or maybe it was just the motion of the boat drawing their faces together. Or perhaps the fog muted every word, rendering every breath more intimate than it would otherwise have been. Because suddenly his mouth was hovering mere millimetres over hers, then even closer, his warm breath mingling with her pale puffs of air, and then his lips met hers and her world tilted on its axis.

He had soft lips. In a face that looked as if it had been chiselled from stone she hadn't expected that. Nor tenderness, surprising in its sweetness. But there was warmth and heat and the feel of his long-fingered hands through her hair. The combination was lethal.

Time stood still. The chugging of the engine

disappeared under the *whump-whump* of her own heartbeat in her ears. The world was reduced to this boat, to this one man and one woman and the magic swirling like the fog around them. She sighed into him, melting as his mouth moved over hers, parting her lips so that she could taste him, and his kiss deepened, his tongue tracing the line of her teeth, duelling with hers.

He tasted of coffee and liqueur, leather and man, and underneath was another layer which was heat and strength and desire, and she wanted more.

This was a kiss—not a mere peck on the cheek like he'd given her earlier. This was a kiss that spun her senses out of control, a kiss that melted her bones and short-circuited her brain.

When finally they drew apart her knees were trembling and her breathing was ragged, as though she'd run a sprint.

'Rosa…' he whispered in her hair. His breathing was coming fast too, and she could see that he had also been affected by their kiss. 'I'm so sorry.'

'You're sorry that you kissed me?'

He made a sound, like a laugh. 'Oh, no. I'm not sorry for that. Not sorry at all.'

'That's good,' she said, still clinging to him, afraid that if she let go he might take his arms away and her legs wouldn't have the strength to hold her up. 'I think…' she started. 'I think that I forgive you.'

'You do?'

'But only on one condition.'

'Name it.'

'Only if you kiss me again.'

He growled.

To Rosa it sounded like a cry of triumph, of victory, as he swept her up in his arms and twirled her around so that her feet left the deck. At any other time she would have been fearful of falling out of the vessel, but not now. With Vittorio's strong arms around her she felt that nothing could go wrong. And when he put her down his big hands were cupping her face.

'I dreamed about this,' he said.

She was breathless all over again. 'You dreamed about kissing me?'

'More. I dreamed about spending the rest of the night with you.'

She gasped. There was no way she could prevent it. It was as involuntary as the flip of her stomach and the sudden clench of muscles between her thighs she'd never realised existed.

'But that's up to you. Let's see about my earning your forgiveness first.'

His mouth descended once more. She felt the tickle of his falling hair around her face, the graze of his whiskered cheeks and the exquisite, unexpected softness of his lips as his mouth met hers.

He took it slowly. He nibbled and suckled at her lips, teased her tongue with his and beckoned hers into the heated cavern of his mouth; he reassured the rest of her body that it wasn't missing out by sending his hands underneath the cloaks and sweeping them in arcs from her shoulders to the curve of her behind, and if forgiveness could truly be earned in a kiss he was earning a lifetime's worth.

But the kiss didn't end there. He changed gear, ratcheting up from gentle and considerate to plundering. Demanding. And she gave herself up to passion and to a heat such as she'd never known. She was burning up from the inside out.

Tiny details assumed major status. The precise angle of his mouth over hers, the puff of his breath on her cheek, the creak of leather as his arms moved around her. Tiny things, insignificant in themselves, and yet all part of something major, something momentous. Her breasts were straining tight inside her bodice, her nipples ached, and all she knew, with the tiny part of her brain that was still functioning, was that she never wanted these feelings to end.

Was it magic? Or merely lust?

She didn't care.

What did it matter when it felt this good?

By the time his head drew back she was lost to it. They could have fallen into the dark and frigid waters of the canal and she would have noticed nothing—not even the steam that would have come from their union.

'Make love to me, Rosa.' His breathing was rushed and ragged, his voice no more than a rasp on the night air. 'Spend the night with me.'

A spike of fear made its presence known—an age-old fear that she'd carried with her all her womanly life—and despite her earlier fantasies about the magic of the night that fear reared its head.

Sure, she wasn't completely naïve. She knew how things were supposed to work. But what did she really know of the intimacy of the bedroom? What if she couldn't? What if she did something wrong? What if it hurt? What if she made a fool of herself?

But those fears were no match for the arousal that spiralled up from within and surrounded her. Like a suit of armour, it protected her from her fears. There were still curling tendrils of doubt, but they were all but blunted, making room for anticipation and heady excitement, because this night would be a night like no other.

And somehow she knew she couldn't be in better hands.

She sucked in a breath while he waited for her

answer, needing the cold night air to cool her while it could. 'I'd like that,' she said, and he gave a low growl of approval in his throat.

He took a moment to yell instructions to the driver and she had a sense of the boat changing direction as he turned her face up to his for another kiss.

Maybe it was just lust, Rosa thought as he pulled her against his mouth.

But there was magic happening tonight too.

Pure magic.

CHAPTER FIVE

FROM THE FIRST moment their eyes had met Rosa had recognised that there was something about this man, something magnetic that had drawn her towards him, something commanding. But something that scared her, too. There was an edge to him, as though if she ventured too close she might fall.

And yet she'd agreed to spend the night with him.

But now, stepping from the deck of the motor-boat and into a building, she felt a further sense of unease. Because it wasn't any ordinary building.

'What is this place?' she asked as he led her by the hand towards a flight of stairs. It was not a hotel, as she'd been expecting. And it was no humble apartment. 'Is this your home?'

'What? Here in Venice? No,' he said dismissively. 'It's a private residence. I just get to stay here occasionally.'

He shrugged, as if having access in any capacity to a *palazzo* on the Grand Canal was nothing special.

Rosa looked around. Maybe this *palazzo* didn't quite rival Marcello's in grandeur, but it was still very definitely a *palazzo*, and it was filled with treasures of Murano glass, sculptures, chandeliers and gilt everything.

'So where *do* you live?' she asked, her heels tapping on the marble staircase.

'North of here. Near the border with Slovenia.'

'Near Trieste?'

He turned to her and smiled. 'Do you always ask this many questions when you're nervous.'

'I'm not nervous,' she lied on a lilting laugh.

But a few moments later he opened the door to a bedroom and her heart all but jumped out of her chest with nerves.

He dimmed the lights, but there was no dimming the vision that met her eyes, because across the room was a wide bed—impossibly wide. She swallowed. There was only one place this could end, and she wanted it, but still…

'Would you like something to drink?' he offered, already stripping away her armour of cloaks, peeling away her courage at the same time. 'Prosecco or another spritz?'

She shook her head. She didn't need more alcohol, or anything with bubbles. There was already too much fizzing going on in her blood.

'Then water.'

He pulled a bottle of water from a cabinet and poured them both a glass. She accepted it, more to give herself something to do with her hands rather than because her throat was suddenly desert-dry.

She was still contemplating that bed. She knew what the act entailed, but why was there no guide-book for the prelude? *Dio*, she really hoped she didn't mess this up.

She heard the soft tap of his glass being put down on a cabinet behind her, and then a sound that could only be the unbuckling of his leather trousers and a long zipper being undone. She clutched her glass with both hands.

Help!

'Rosa…' he said as he gently took her arm and turned her towards him.

He was bare-chested, dressed only in the leather of his costume pants. Her hungry eyes could not help but drink in the muscular perfection of his shoulders, his chest and his sculpted abdomen. She'd thought him perfect wrapped in leather of blue and gold, but now, dressed only in a pair of leather trousers slung low over his hips, he looked even more magnificent.

Breathtaking. Heart stopping.

Terrifying.

He smiled, then eased the glass from her tangled fingers and put it aside. 'Now,' he said, as he put his hands to her neck and eased her hair back over her shoulders. 'Where were we?'

Her mind was a blank. She had no idea what he was talking about, let alone how to answer.

But his warm hands answered his question for her, meeting at the nape of her neck and drawing her closer to him. Closer to his intense blue eyes. Closer to his parted, waiting lips.

She felt the heat of his mouth, the warmth of his hands at the back of her head, holding her to him. She felt the heat of his body even before he drew her still closer and her breasts met the hard wall of his chest as he deepened the kiss.

Her breasts ached for release. Her nipples were pressing hard against a suddenly too tight bodice as her blood swirled drunkenly around her veins. Her legs felt boneless and she had to put her hands to his chest to steady herself. But once they were there steadying herself against his body was the lesser priority. She needed to feel him, to drink in the texture of his sculpted body, to see if he felt as good as he looked.

And he did. He was magnificent, his body a landscape of contrasts. Hard muscles. Smooth skin. Wiry tangle of chest hair. Firm nub of nipples. But the realisation only ramped up both her desire and her nervousness.

'You're trembling...' He breathed rather than said the words as his lips worked the soft folds and ridges of her ears, his breath fanning like a musical breeze against her skin. 'Are you cold?'

Anything but. She was alight with fire, flames were burning her up from within, breathing life into the coals that already glowed hot deep down in the pit of her belly.

'No…' she whispered on a gasp of oxygen, and that tiny, one-syllable word was all she was capable of before his mouth once against captured hers and she was sucked back into the vortex of his kiss.

Was it possible to spin any more out of control?

Yes, she realised when she felt his fingers tug on the pull of her zip. Clever fingers to find such a well-disguised invisible zip, but even the knowledge that he was a man used to finding his way into women's clothing couldn't stop another rushing tide of heat as her dress loosened around her and threatened to fall away.

And, then like the burst of cool air that swirled into the exposed space at her back, a surge of panic saw her hands fold over her breasts. She wasn't wearing a bra and there would be nothing between them…

It was too late, and she realised how unsophisticated it must make her look, but all she could do was clutch her dress to her all the harder.

'So shy,' he said with a smile. 'Anyone would think…'

She turned her head away, but not before he'd

seen the truth she tried to hide skittering across her eyes and the heated blush flooding her skin.

'No...' he said, and when she dared look back she saw disbelief mixed with something that looked like horror in his eyes. 'But you *can't* be a virgin. How old are you?'

'I'm sorry,' she said, wanting to run away. 'I didn't realise virginity came with a use-by date.'

He let her go and stepped away. Ran a hand through his hair. A *virgin*! Why the hell hadn't he picked up on it? She'd been like a startled doe trapped in the headlights from the start—flighty and nervous and blushing like a school-girl. And desperate to point out that she was no courtesan. All the clues had been there and yet he'd been too blind to see what had been staring him in the face.

He turned and she was still standing there, holding her dress to her breasts like a shield. 'Rosa,' he said, 'why didn't you tell me? You should have told me.'

'When should I have done that, exactly? When you found me lost in the square and you asked my name? Or when you were kissing me on the motorboat and asked me to make love to you? When would have been the best time to slip my lack of sexual expertise casually into the conversation?'

She had a point. But a *virgin*?

He shook his head. Virgins were trouble. They had expectations. It wasn't a sacrifice most made lightly—parting with the known and the safe for the unknown. They took the act of love as an act of sharing and a promise of commitment. They had hopes and dreams he had no way of fulfilling.

'Look—' he said, shaking his head.

'I'm sorry,' she said cutting him off. 'You asked me to spend the night with you.' The end of her tongue found her lips. 'I said yes. So why should this make a difference?'

'It's your first time,' he replied. 'You don't want to waste it on a one-night stand. And that's all it will be, Rosa. That's all it can ever be—one night. I can't offer you any more than that.'

'I just want to finish what you started. I don't want any more than that.'

No? That was what they all said, and then afterwards would come the tears.

'Rosa—'

'Please,' she said. 'I really want to. I'm just a bit nervous, that's all.'

She took a deep breath, then took her hands away from her dress and let it crumple to the floor, standing naked before him but for her panties.

Breath hissed through his teeth. *Dio*, but she was beautiful. Curvy, with dark-tipped breasts and a narrow waist that begged a man to run his

hands down the sides, to drink them in, to feel for himself the exquisite flare of her hips.

An erection he thought had been banished by her revelation kicked back into life with a vengeance.

'Are you sure about this?' he asked, taking a step closer. Because she needed to be certain.

'I'm sure,' she said. 'What do you want me to do?'

'Oh, Rosa,' he said as he swung her into his arms, 'Your first time—all I want you to do is feel and enjoy.'

He laid her on the bed and sat beside her, held her face in his hands and kissed her gently on the mouth.

She was so nervous, her skin alive to sensation and his every touch like a brand, but he stilled her with his kiss. Soothed her.

'Don't be afraid,' he said, as if he could see inside her.

She smiled tremulously up at him and he kissed her again before dipping his mouth lower, kissing her throat, her collarbones, her shoulders, then kissing first one peaked nipple and then the other.

'So beautiful,' he said, and returned to her mouth, his kiss deeper, giving and taking more.

Her hands moved of their own volition, wanting to feel, to explore. His muscles bunched and shifted under her hands, and every touch, every texture, fed into her need, adding to the mix bubbling in the cauldron inside her.

She'd thought it would be quick, that it would be over soon. But he took his time exploring her body with his hot mouth and his clever fingers, until every nerve-ending in her body felt as if it was about to explode. When he drew down her underwear and touched a hand to her mound, one finger sliding between her slick folds, she almost did. Then and only then he stood and peeled down his leather trousers.

His erection sprang free and she gasped, feeling a momentary spike of panic. He was too big… there was no way… But then he was back, kissing her, and she could feel him hard against her belly, and she knew she wanted him inside her— whatever it took.

Still he didn't rush. Her body was burning up with need. She was panting with it, desperate, searching for relief, when he reached for a packet on the bedside table. He ripped it open and knelt above her, sliding protection down his long length. So long…

And then he was there, nudging at her entrance and sending those acutely sensitive nerve-endings into a frenzy. He kissed her deeply, opening her to him, his tongue plundering as he raised one of her legs over his hip and plunged into her.

Stars exploded behind her eyes. Stars that sent shimmering fragments whirling around the delicious feeling of fullness at her core.

He held himself still, his words coming in heady gasps. 'Are you all right?'

She remembered how to breathe, drawing in a ragged breath. 'I'm good,' she managed.

He started to move, to withdraw, and she missed him already. Newly found muscles clamped down, trying to hold on to him, and just when she thought he was lost to her he was back, and she was better than good.

He picked up the rhythm and in the friction he generated she found her stars again, this time strewn on the surface of the sea, wave after wave of shimmering sensation building inside her with every thrust. She was tossed higher and higher, faster and faster, until with one final plunge the star-filled waves crashed over her and washed her bonelessly to the shore.

She came back from the delicious place he'd sent her to slowly. Reluctantly. She wondered why the world in front of her eyes seemed so much the same as it had been before when everything had irrevocably shifted.

She'd expected to feel different. Regretful. Maybe even a little sad.

Instead, she felt…*good*.

Vittorio lay breathing hard next to her, his body

hot, his skin slick with sweat. He lifted his head and kissed her cheek. 'Did I hurt you? Are you okay?'

She smiled and shook her head. There'd been a momentary flash of pain, but it had been lost in a shower storm of stars.

She kissed him back. 'Thank you. That was nice.'

His eyebrows shot up. *'Nice?'* he growled as he rolled out of bed to pad to the bathroom.

She grinned and scooted up the bed, slipping under the covers to hide her naked body. It was insane, after what they'd just done, but with him gone she felt exposed again.

'Very nice?'

She heard him chuckle and then he returned, sliding into the bed alongside her.

'Oh,' she said, unsure of the protocol. 'Should I go home now?'

'I promised you one night,' he said, settling her into the crook of his shoulder so he could dip his head to kiss her again. 'We might as well make the most of it.'

It was later, much later, and Vittorio's body was humming its way down from another crescendo. Rosa's fingernails were idly stroking his chest, and she asked, 'What happened to the kitten you rescued?'

He'd been so lulled by the rhythmic strokes of her fingernails, making swirls in the hair on his chest, that he almost missed the question.

'What?'

'The one you pulled from the bag in the stream.'

'You heard that?'

'I was nearly at the stairs when I saw Sirena was talking to you and Marcello. What happened to it? Did you keep it?'

'I took it to the housekeeper.'

He thought back. There would have been no point taking it to his father. His father would have told him that he was his mother's son and therefore weak—too weak to be the heir to the throne.

'My father would have told me to show some backbone for once in my life and throw the wretched thing back where I'd found it.'

But Maria had cried when she'd heard his story and she'd taken it and cuddled it before setting about finding it some bread to soak in milk.

'She kept it in the kitchen to keep down the mice.'

The thick medieval castle walls had shifted so often over the centuries, and been renovated so many times, it was impossible to plug all the tiny hidey holes. He'd often arrived in the kitchen to find Maria breathless as she chased after another mouse with her straw broom across the flagstones.

'You had your own housekeeper?'

'*Que?*' Too late he realised he'd almost given too much away, but this woman had a way of breaking down his defences. Of disarming him. 'Oh. After my mother died…'

'Of course,' she said, filling in the blanks as she understood them, relieving him of the need to finish while the circles of her fingers grew larger, sweeping lower over his abs. 'Somebody had to look after you both.'

'Somebody had to,' he agreed, lulled by the caress of her nails on his skin.

Maria had looked after them, along with a *castello* full of staff and courtiers and advisers. For a moment he felt guilty that he couldn't tell her, and that once again he was keeping secrets from her. But it wouldn't be the same if she knew. It would change things. It always did. It was better to leave it the way she understood it to be—that he was a friend of someone whose family had once been something important in Venice.

'Your father sounds very controlling. I mean, not just the kitten, but expecting you to marry who he chooses.'

He gave a low snort. 'That's one word for it. But I've been married. It ended badly.'

'Oh, I didn't know. I'm sorry.'

'It's not your fault,' he said, and she chuckled

as both of them remembered their earlier conversation.

'Some families are like that, though, aren't they?' she said. 'Expecting to stage-manage their children's lives, maybe even wanting them to live the life they couldn't.'

He nodded, feeling the caress of her fingertips like a balm to his soul. 'What about your family, Rosa?' He smiled apologetically. 'Your *papà*, I mean. What's he like?'

'Wonderful. He's the one who urged me to leave home and find work somewhere else. I was happy at home—it was nice taking care of the house for everyone after Mamma died—but one by one my brothers married and left home, and eventually there was just my *papà* and me. He told me that if I didn't leave home and the village I'd never see anything of the world, and I'd be stuck looking after him when he got old.'

Her hand stopped and her head lifted.

'I don't think I should be talking about my father right now.'

He patted her shoulder. 'My fault,' he said, wondering why he had asked. He didn't need to know anything more about Rosa than what she'd brought to this bed. He didn't need to know about her family. He didn't want to hear it. 'Let's talk about something else.'

'Talk?' she said, her fingertips back in action and growing bolder, her nails raking circles around his navel, swooping in and out. Teasing. Taunting.

His loins stirred. 'You've got a better idea?' he asked, his voice laced with a gravel edge.

Her fingertips edged lower, gliding over his tip. Her courage was growing by the minute. She'd always been a quick learner.

'Could we, do you think…? Just once more?'

Could we? He was suddenly harder than the question was to answer. But he had to remember she was new at this. Brave, curious, but inexperienced.

'You're not too sore?'

She shook her head, her fingers encircling him. Stroking him.

'Right now I'd like you to make love to me again,' she said. 'I can be sore tomorrow.'

CHAPTER SIX

VITTORIO WOKE TO watery sunlight slipping through the gaps in the heavy brocade drapes, a supreme sense of satisfaction and a goodly measure of anticipation. But sunlight…? So the fog had lifted.

He rolled over on his back and reached out an arm, searching for the source of his satisfaction and the reason for his anticipation, only to find the other side of the bed empty and the sheets cold.

What the…?

He rose up on his elbows. 'Rosa?' he called into the gloom, his eyes scanning the room, searching for any evidence of her.

But the chair where he'd flung her dress after he'd peeled it off was empty and the rug where he'd placed her shoes after he'd slipped them off was bare. There was only his rapidly discarded leather trousers littering the floor.

'Rosa!' he called, louder this time, swiping back the covers to pad barefoot across the carpet to the bathroom. But that room was dark and empty too.

She was gone.

He headed back to the bedroom, sat on the side of the bed and picked up his watch from the side table. Almost noon. *Dio*, what time had they got to sleep? The last thing he could remember thinking was that he would shut his eyes for ten minutes to recover—and then he didn't remember thinking anything at all.

He put his head in his hands and thought back. She'd said something about working today. He'd wondered at the time if it had just been an excuse to escape the party, but she'd told him she was a cleaner in a three-star hotel. Maybe she *did* have to work. Which meant… What godawful time must she have left?

He stood up on a sigh and headed back to the bathroom, swiping open the nearest curtains on the way. Milky light spilled into the room, banishing the gloom, while outside, if Venice had a hangover it didn't show.

Venice was getting on with being Venice. *Vaporettos* and gondolas alike were ferrying tourists backwards and forwards, rubbish barges filled with last night's garbage were skulking out of the way as a water ambulance screamed along the canal.

He had to get back to Andachstein.

Even so, he thought as he looked at his face in the bathroom mirror, his hands stroking his rough jaw, it was disappointing that she'd cut and run before he could make love to her one last time.

He stepped under the rain-shower spray, sighing in approval as he turned his face into the hot water and felt it cascade down his body. Just because he was in a fifteenth-century *palazzo* it didn't mean he had to go without modern plumbing.

He smiled to himself. A virgin. Rosa had started out so shy and timid and then turned to liquid mercury in his arms, as sinuous as the canal that weaved its way outside his windows. One spark and she'd sizzled with sensuality, turning an otherwise dark night into a blaze of heat and passion.

He'd been honest—at least as far as commitment went. He'd laid all his cards on the table. One night and one night only, and definitely no chance of for ever. So it was probably for the best that she'd already gone. It avoided any of those awkward post-coital conversations when last night's warnings tended to get somehow twisted by the act of intercourse, when words took on a different meaning from how they'd been intended and first understood.

How many times had he heard the same old arguments? *'But that was before you made love to me...'* and *'I thought you cared about me...'*

At least she'd saved them both that anguish.

He roughly towelled himself off and dropped his towel on the floor as he headed for the dressing room. A virgin. How about that? It had been a long time since he'd encountered a virgin. He didn't tend to move in the same circles as teenagers or gauche twenty-somethings.

She'd made him laugh. And she'd been perfectly right. It wasn't as if virginity self-destructed if you didn't use it up. It was just that most people he knew seemed to have found a way to dispense with it before they'd abandoned their teens.

He had his underwear and trousers on, and had just pulled a white shirt from a hanger, was reefing it over his shoulders, when he saw it. A glint of something gold amidst the tangle of linen and coverlets on the bed. His eyes narrowed. A trick of the watery light?

He moved closer as he buttoned his shirt. No. There was definitely something there. Something small.

He reached down and picked it up and realised what it was as the pearl swung free on the ring that attached it to a golden stud. One of Rosa's earrings.

She'd left it here.

On purpose?

The moment the thought popped into his mind he discarded it. He was far too world-weary. While plenty of women he'd met would,

Rosa wouldn't play games like that. She wasn't the type.

It looked old. She would be sure to miss it.

He should return it. There were no excuses. He knew where she worked.

He should give it to the housekeeper and have it delivered. Rosa would have it back in a matter of hours.

He should return it.

He twirled the delicate earring in his fingers, held it to his nose as if by doing so he could conjure up her scent.

He should return it.

His fingers closed around it where it lay in his palm and he slipped it into his trouser pocket.

He would return it.

Later.

CHAPTER SEVEN

'WHERE DID YOU get to?' Chiara cried, bolting up-right in bed and turning on her bedside lamp the second Rosa walked into the tiny basement flat the girls shared. 'I've been worried sick about you.'

'I got lost,' Rosa said, checking the time on the alarm clock glowing red. Four-thirty a.m.

She unzipped her gown and let it slip down her body for the second time that night, shivering at the memory of the first. She would have time for an hour's sleep if she put her head down on her pillow right now.

Sleep? After what she'd experienced tonight? She might be kidding herself about that. But at least she'd have an hour to savour the memories.

'I'm really sorry I suggested carrying your phone for you,' Chiara said, watching her pre-pare for bed. 'I feel so bad for ruining your night.'

'Don't worry about it. How was the ball?'

'So much fun,' she said, and her face lit up be-fore she could think better of it. 'I tried to find you. We searched and searched and I called the hotel in case you'd come back, but nobody had seen you. I didn't expect to be home before you.'

'It's okay. Forget it.'

'So where were you?'

'I met someone,' Rosa said, sliding between the sheets. 'He invited me to a party he was going to.'

'He? A man? You went to a party with a stranger?' Chiara was all agog. She swung her legs out of bed and sat up. *'You?'*

Rosa didn't take offence at her friend's surprise. She knew what she meant.

'What was he like?'

'Oh, Chiara...' Rosa sighed, propping herself up on her elbow, head resting on her hand. 'You should have seen him. He was tall, and strong, and... I wouldn't call him really handsome—but powerful-looking. With the most amazing blue eyes I've ever seen.'

'What was his name?'

'Vittorio.' Even now the sound of it on her tongue was delicious.

'And he asked you to go to a party with him?'

She smiled. *'Si.'*

'Why?'

Rosa shrugged. This part could do with a bit of airbrushing of the truth. She plucked at some imaginary fluff on her sheet. 'He felt sorry for me that I was missing my costume ball after I'd spent so much money on a ticket.'

'And there *was* a party, I hope?'

'Oh, yes. In this amazing *palazzo* right on the

Grand Canal. It even had a second *piano nobile*— can you imagine? The party was on the second level and the first level was set up with the entertainment. They had music and jugglers and opera singers, and even gymnasts performing on ropes. It was amazing. And you should have seen the costumes, Chiara! *Amazing.*' Rosa punched her pillow and settled down. 'Can you turn off the light? We have to get up soon.'

'And you were at this party all night, then?'

'Uh-huh. Turn off the light.'

'And then you came home?'

'I'm tired,' Rosa said, hugging her precious secret to her, not willing to share just yet. She might tell Chiara one day about what had really happened. Maybe. 'And we've got to be up in less than an hour.'

Chiara sniffed and extinguished the light, clearly recognising the sense in Rosa's words and the fact she was not going to hear any more tonight.

'All right, have it your way. But I want all the details tomorrow!'

'Goodnight,' said Rosa noncommittally, snuggling into her pillow, and only then noticing the press of her earring stud into her flesh. In her rush to get to bed she'd forgotten to take her earrings off. She removed the offending article and reached for the one on the other side—only to find it gone.

She sat up, switching on the lamp.

'What now?' said Chiara grumpily. 'I thought you wanted to go to sleep?'

'I can't find one of my earrings.' Her eyes searched the floor around the bed. She got out and shook her dress, in case she'd dislodged it when she'd pulled the gown over her head. But of course it wasn't there, because she hadn't done that at all.

'Go to bed.'

'They were my grandmother's,' she said. 'A gift from my grandfather on their wedding day.' And, apart from her mother's sewing machine, they were the only thing of real value she had.

'Go to bed!' Chiara repeated grumpily. 'Look for it tomorrow.'

'But—'

'Turn off the light!'

Rosa did a quick sweep with her hands of her bedding and her pillow before she complied and climbed back into bed. She switched off the light and settled back down.

Where could it be? She'd been wearing them both at Vittorio's. She remembered seeing them when she'd looked in the mirror in the bathroom. But that had been before…

Dio. But at least if it was there someone might find it—a cleaner or a housekeeper—and she might be able to get it back. Better that than thinking it had fallen out on her way home somewhere along the twisty *calles.*

Either way, if she couldn't find it here she'd go looking after her shift tomorrow—*today*.

One night only.

She thought about Vittorio's warning that one night was all there would be, that it wasn't an affair and he didn't do for ever. If he was at home she wouldn't pester him. She wouldn't ask for him. She just wanted her earring back, if it had been found. And if he learned she had visited he'd understand why she'd had to come back. She was sure he would.

So she'd retrace her steps to his *palazzo*, and if she didn't find it on the way she'd knock on the door. There was no harm in asking, surely?

Rosa was almost overcome with exhaustion by the time she finished her shift. She'd been exhausted before she'd started, though for an entirely different reason, but by the end of the shift it was pure drudgery weighing her down. It seemed every visitor had hung around until the end of Carnevale and then checked out today, which had meant changeovers in almost every room.

By the time she was finished all she wanted to do was collapse in a heap in her bed. Except that wouldn't get her pearl earring back, so she changed into jeans and a jacket and headed out into the tortuous *calles* of Venice once again, trying to retrace her steps.

It was no wonder she took a wrong turn once or twice—she was so busy looking at the ground in front of her—but eventually she found it: the gate where she'd made her escape that morning from Vittorio's *palazzo*. She rang the buzzer and waited. And waited.

She rang the buzzer again.

Eventually the door opened to reveal a stern-looking middle-aged woman. 'This is a private residence. We're not open to visitors.'

'No,' Rosa said, before the woman could shut the door as abruptly as she'd opened it. 'I was here last night. I lost an earring.'

The woman shook her head. 'I think you have the wrong residence.' She started closing the gate again.

'I was with Vittorio,' Rosa said. 'I don't want to bother him, but it was my grandmother's earring, given to her on her wedding day. I think I may have lost it here, and if I could get it back…'

The woman sniffed as she opened the gate a fraction more, looking Rosa up and down as if finding her story hard to believe and yet not impossible. 'Vittorio is no longer here. I don't know when he'll be back. He's not in Venice very often.'

'I didn't come to see Vittorio,' said Rosa. 'It's my grandmother's earring I'm looking for. That's all. I promise.'

The woman sighed. 'Then I'm sorry. I can't

help you, I'm afraid. I cleaned that room myself. Nothing was found.'

And she eased the door shut in Rosa's face.

It could have been worse, Rosa thought, heading home, still checking the ground in case her earring had come loose during the evening and fallen out on the way home. The housekeeper might have practically slammed the door in her face but at least she'd listened to her. At least she knew she hadn't lost it there.

'I'm sorry, Nonna,' she said as she got closer to home and there was still no sight of the missing earring. 'I'm sorry I didn't take better care of it for you.'

The streets had no answer.

It was gone.

She'd thought she'd got off scot-free, but maybe this was the price she had to pay, Rosa rationalised as she dragged herself back to the hotel and her tiny basement flat and home to bed. For nothing came without a cost. She knew that.

Maybe one lost earring was the price she had to pay for one night of sin.

And the worst part of it was her night with Vittorio had been so special, so once-in-a-lifetime, she almost felt the loss of one of her grandmother's earrings was worth it.

CHAPTER EIGHT

THE SUMMONS FROM his father's secretary came within five minutes of Vittorio's arrival back at the *castello*. Vittorio snorted as he settled back into his rooms. Some things never changed. His father had never once come to *him*, let alone met him at the castle doors when he'd returned from being away. Not when he'd come home as a child on holiday from boarding school in Switzerland. Not when he'd come home after three years of college in Boston.

Although there was something to be said for knowing how a person worked. You knew exactly how to press their hot buttons.

'At last,' his father said when Vittorio arrived thirty minutes after the summons.

On the Guglielmo Richter Scale, as Vittorio had termed it as a boy, his father seemed to be in good spirits, and he wondered if he shouldn't have taken longer to accede to his father's request.

'I've been waiting for news. I thought you might have had the decency to let me know before now, but now that you're finally here tell me everything.' Prince Guglielmo clearly enunciated his demands as he wandered from one side of his office to the other. In his blue double-breasted jacket, and with one hand tucked behind his back, he looked as if he was inspecting the guard.

Through the vast windows behind him Vittorio could see down to the glorious sweep of Andachstein coast that separated Italy from Slovenia, and the swarm of white yachts that lay at anchor in the protected harbour while their occupants entertained themselves in the casinos, clubs and restaurants that lined the white sand beaches. Even at the tail end of winter they came in their droves—the rich and famous, the billionaires and their mistresses, the actors and actresses. The only difference was that in summertime it would be a sea of white and there wouldn't be a spare berth anywhere.

His father stopped pacing.

'Well? Have you set a date?' the older Prince prompted. 'Can we alert the press, the public? I need to get Enrico on to it immediately, before the news leaks from other sources.'

Other sources. Clearly his father didn't trust Sirena to keep a secret. If there had been one to keep. But he didn't say that. Instead he frowned and said, 'Have I set a date…?' He was being deliberately obtuse, playing the game.

His father snorted, impatience winning over civility, edging him higher up the Guglielmo Richter Scale. 'You and the Contessa Sirena, of course.

Who else?' He fixed his son with a gimlet stare. 'Have you agreed a date?'

Vittorio picked up a paperweight from his father's desk—a crystal dragon, symbol of the principality—and tossed it casually from one hand to the other. He saw his father's eyes follow the object that he'd been forbidden to touch as a child. He half expected him to snap now, tell him to put it down in case he dropped it, as he had then. But his father said nothing and Vittorio sighed. It was time to put his father out of his misery.

He put the paperweight down and leant with both hands against the desk, wanting no distractions when he delivered his message. 'There is no date. There will be no marriage. At least not between Sirena and me.'

'What?'

His father's voice boomed so loud in the cavernous room that Vittorio swore the windows rattled.

'When are you going to take your responsibilities seriously?'

'There's no rush.'

'There *is* a rush! It was all supposed to be organised. You two were supposed to come to an agreement. All you had to do was set a date and it seems you can't even be trusted to do that.'

'Actually, I have an idea,' Vittorio suggested. 'If you're so desperate to welcome Sirena into the family business, why don't you marry her yourself?'

His father spluttered and banged his fist on the desk. 'You damned well know this isn't about the Contessa. This is about providing Andachstein with an heir. Without a prince there can be no principality. Andachstein will be swallowed up into the realm of Italy.' He looked his son up and down with disdain. 'You might like to think you're invincible, my son, but you won't last for ever, you know.'

'Look, Father,' he said with a sigh. 'It will happen. I will marry again. But don't expect that I'm going to fall in with your plans just because it's what you want. And don't make such a big deal out of it.'

'I'm *dying*!' Guglielmo blurted, his face beet-root-red.

The son who had grown up with a father who had always used drama to bend the people around him to his will said, 'We're all dying, Father.'

'Insolence!'

'I'm thirty-two years old. I'm not a child, even if I am your son. So if you've got something to tell me then simply tell me.'

'Heart problems.' His father spat out the words.

Heart problems? But that would mean... Vittorio bit back on the obvious retort while his father waved his hands around, looking for words.

'Something to do with the valves,' his father said, 'I forget the name. So fix it, I told the doctors. Replace them. And they told me that while one of them was operable the other was more problematic. They say it is fifty-fifty that I would survive the operation. Without it they say I most likely have less than a year to live.'

Guglielmo collapsed into the chair behind his desk, suddenly weary, and Vittorio noticed that he looked more like an eighty-year-old, rather than the sixty he was supposed to be.

'I've decided to take my chance on life,' he said, 'rather than on some cold operating table.' He turned to his son. 'But I want you married before I die, whatever happens.'

'Dio,' Vittorio said, with the shock of realisation reverberating through his body. 'You're actually serious.'

'Of course I'm serious!' he said. 'And I have a son who won't face up to his responsibilities and do what his duty demands of him.'

Vittorio's hands fisted at his sides. Dying or no, his father was not getting away with that one. 'I faced up to my responsibilities once before. Don't you remember? And look how that turned out!'

His father waved his arguments aside. 'Valentina was weak. She was a bad choice.'

'She was *your* choice,' Vittorio snarled.

His father had decided on the match before

the two had even been introduced. The first time they'd met Vittorio had been smitten. She'd seemed like a bright and beautiful butterfly and he'd fallen instantly and irrevocably in love with her. And he'd believed her when she told him that she loved him.

But she had been young and impressionable, and he'd been too foolish to see what was in front of his face. That the family helicopter pilot she'd insisted move with her to the *castello* at Andachstein, so that she could continue her flying lessons, was teaching her a whole lot more than how to handle a helicopter...

He would never forgive himself for not talking her out of leaving with her lover after he'd confronted her with the knowledge that they'd been seen together. He'd been too gutted. Too devastated. He'd loved her so much and she'd betrayed him, and so he'd let her run distraught to her pilot and escape, tears streaming down her face.

He'd never been sure who had been at the controls when they'd hit the powerlines that had ended their lives.

'*Dio*, Father, don't you understand why I don't want you to have anything to do with choosing another bride for me?'

It was as much about getting out from under his father's thumb as it was about the fact that he'd sworn never to be such a fool again. Never to trust a woman's lies. Never to let his heart control his decisions.

His father mumbled something under his breath. Something mostly incoherent. But Vittorio was sure he heard the word *ungrateful* in the mix.

'Well,' he said, 'something has to be done and I don't have long to wait. I'm giving you three months.'

'What?'

'Three months should be perfectly adequate. Find your own bride, if you must, but you're getting married in the Andachstein Cathedral in three months and that's my final word. I'll have Enrico make a list of the best candidates.'

His father couldn't be serious. But then, Vittorio had thought he was joking about dying. *Heart problems. A year to live.* If it were true, Vittorio would be the new Prince of Andachstein, not just the heir apparent.

The ground shifted under his feet. Longevity ran through the line of Andachstein Princes—the last had died at ninety-seven. The youngest ever to die had been seventy-eight. He'd imagined his father, in these modern medicine times, had at least another twenty years to run down on his body clock.

'No,' Vittorio said, and his father's head jerked up, as if Vittorio was rejecting his demand out of hand. 'Not Enrico,' he said. His father's secretary had just as poor judgement for who would make a good wife as his father did. 'I'll get Marcello to help me.'

His father cocked one wiry eyebrow. 'She needs to be the right kind of woman,' he said. 'With the right family connections.'

'Of course.'

'Not to mention good breeding stock.'

Vittorio almost raised a smile. He wasn't entirely sure how he was supposed to assess that, but he simply said, 'Next you'll be insisting she's a virgin.'

The older man looked over at him. 'I may be dying, but I'm not stupid. The search will be difficult enough without making it impossible.'

This time Vittorio did smile. There was no way he wasn't trying before buying.

His father nodded, taking his son's smile as agreement, seemingly satisfied with how the meeting had gone. 'You have three months. Don't let me down. I would very much like to meet the next Princess of Andachstein before I die.' His voice cracked on the final word and he put his head down and gave a dismissive wave of his hand. 'Now, leave me.'

Vittorio nodded, and left his father at his desk, and as he walked down the long corridor that led from his father's official rooms to his own apartment he wondered about the glint that he'd seen in his father's eyes.

Tears?

It hardly seemed possible. He'd never seen his father cry. Not when they'd been sitting at the bedside of his wife of thirty years and she'd given up her last breath and slipped silently away. Not even when they'd interred her in the family crypt and the hound she had loved for twelve years had howled uncontrollably and mournfully at their feet, as if he knew he'd just lost his best friend. Every other mourner except his father had lost it right then.

But tears would mean that his father was almost human.

Was that what knowing you were going to die—having an end date rather than a vague statistic—did to you? Made you confront your own mortality? Made you human?

His father.

Dying.

It was an impossible concept to grasp.

He'd always been closer to his mother. She'd never been warm, exactly—he'd felt far more welcome in the kitchen than in his mother's salon—but she'd been the one who'd held the two men in her life together, and when she'd died the yawning chasm between father and son had widened. And that had been before Valentina had died and the gulf and the resentment between them had grown still wider.

Vittorio was in no hurry to get married again. His experience of marriage was no fond memory. And his parents…? They were hardly shining lights for the institution. No, he was in no hurry.

But he *was* heir to the throne of Andachstein. A position he might be forced to take up long before he had ever imagined. And it *was* his duty to sire an heir.

And, when it all came down to it, Guglielmo was still his father—the only father he'd ever had. So, despite their differences over the years, didn't he owe him something?

Vittorio's footsteps echoed in the old stone stairwell that led up to his apartments the back way. There was a flashier terrazzo-tiled staircase that went the front way, but he preferred the feel of the stone under his feet, the stone steps that held the grooves of the feet of his ancestors and their servants. Ever since he was a child he'd liked stepping into those grooves and wondering how many footsteps it would take to make a dent in the stone. He liked to think he was doing his bit by contributing his own footfall.

Every few steps there was a long narrow window that offered glimpses of the tree-covered hills behind the coast and the city. Once used by archers against marauding invaders, now they were glassed in against the weather. He stopped at one near the top and gazed out over the countryside, not really seeing, just thinking.

Maybe it was time. He was thirty-two and he was tired. Tired of the Sirenas of this world hunting for a title. Tired of the life he was leading.

There had to be something else.

Something more.

It couldn't be too hard to find himself a wife once he set his mind to it, surely? It shouldn't take long to vet the candidates. It wasn't as if he had to go through the motions of falling in love with the woman first.

He'd been in love with Valentina and what a disaster that had turned out to be. But then, was it any wonder? Look at his role models. He wasn't sure his father had ever loved his mother. They'd had separate suites as far back as Vittorio could remember. He'd never once witnessed a display of affection between them.

When it came down to it, it was a miracle he even existed…

CHAPTER NINE

HE CAME OUT of the fog in blue leather trimmed with gold, his long cape swirling in his wake. He emerged tall and broad and powerful, his cobalt eyes zeroing in on her, as if he'd sensed her presence through the mist.

He strode purposefully towards her, stopping bare inches away, so close that she could feel the heat of his body coming at her in waves…so close that she was sure his intense eyes would bore into hers and see inside her very soul.

'Rosa…' he said, in a deep voice that threatened to melt her bones.

'Vittorio,' she said, breathless and trembling, 'you came for me.'

'I had no choice,' he said, and he opened his arms for her.

She stepped into the space he had created just for her and felt his arms ensnare her in his heat and strength as he dipped his head to hers.

Her lips met his. She sighed into his mouth and gave herself up to the delicious heat of his mouth. His tongue. His taste. She felt herself swung into his arms, as if she were weightless, and then time slipped and they were in bed, and he was poised over her, and his name was on her lips as he drove into her…

'*Rosa!*'

The voice was wrong. It didn't fit. It was in the way.

She tried to ignore it. Tried desperately to hang on to what was happening even as the vision wobbled at the edges.

'Stop mooning,' someone said.

Someone who sounded like Chiara.

But what would she be doing at Vittorio's *palazzo*?

'It's time to get up!'

Rosa blinked into wakefulness, feeling a soul-crushing devastation. Feeling cheated. She'd thought Vittorio had come back for her, but it had been nothing but yet another pointless and cruel dream.

'All right,' she said, blinking, getting herself out of bed. 'I'm coming.'

'Forget about him,' Chiara said, brushing her hair.

'Forget about who?'

'Vittorio, of course. He must have been something special for you to dream about him all the time.'

'Who says I was dreaming about him?'

Chiara raised her eyebrows. 'Why else would you call out his name? You've really got it bad.'

Rosa kicked up her chin as she headed for the bathroom. 'I don't know what you're talking about. It was a dream, that's all.'

'When are you going to tell me what happened that night?'

'I told you what happened.'

Chiara just laughed. 'Hurry up,' she said. 'Or you'll be late for work.'

Rosa stepped under the shower spray. How could she share the events of that night with Chiara and convey the magic of the evening without cheapening it? No. She held the secret of what had happened that night like a precious jewel, still too new and too special to share with anyone.

She didn't have stars in her eyes. She wasn't stupid. She knew that despite the dreams that plagued her nights she'd never see Vittorio again. Not that the knowledge stopped her looking out for him every time she ventured anywhere near the Grand Canal. She'd hear a deep voice or see a broad pair of shoulders up ahead and for a split second she'd be hurtled back to that night and think she'd found him again. But the voice always belonged to someone else, and the man with broad shoulders would turn and the likeness would end there.

She didn't mind. He'd told her how it would be. She didn't expect to see him ever again.

He'd just been so wonderful that night. So tender and gentle, so generous in his willingness and desire to ensure her pleasure, so generous in the knowledge he'd shared.

She knew about lovemaking now. She knew what she liked in bed and how to pleasure a man. She had Vittorio to thank for introducing her to the ways of the bedroom.

She didn't really mind that she would never see him again.

She just had a horrible feeling he had ruined her for any other man.

'So this is the list Enrico gave you?'

Marcello looked up and down the three-page printout listing the eligible noblewomen his father's secretary had assembled who might just be persuaded to take on Vittorio and the title of Princess of Andachstein. There was a photograph of each woman alongside her name, together with a sketchy bio giving height, age and weight.

Vittorio snorted. 'I see Enrico's covered all the important details.'

'A veritable smorgasbord of aristocratic talent,' Marcello said drily 'But one thing worries me.'

'What's that?'

'You've only got three months until the date of the wedding. Does that give you enough time to sleep with them all?'

The would-be groom crossed his legs at the

ankles and smirked. Now that he'd made up his mind to fall in with his father's crazy plan and find himself a wife—a princess for Andachstein—he found he liked the idea more and more. An arranged marriage, a convenient marriage—but this time without foolishly falling in love. All he had to do was produce an heir. If the marriage itself floundered after that, so be it. It would be nobody's fault. Nobody would be hurt. It was perfect. Failsafe.

Besides, he was growing tired of his lifestyle. Tired of fighting his destiny. But he wasn't interested in searching for a wife by any other means. So he'd had Enrico clear the appointments that could be cleared, undertaken those that couldn't be avoided, and now, within the space of a week, was sitting in one of the reception rooms in Marcello's *palazzo*.

'Did you see who's at the top of the list?'

Marcello cocked an eyebrow. 'I did notice that. Maybe your father ascribes to the view that it's better the devil you know?'

Vittorio laughed. '*He* might. But I'm not that much of a masochist.' He sat up, forearms on knees, hands clasped. 'So what do you think?'

Marcello flicked between the pages, exhaling long and loud as he shook his head. 'Well, it's not the list *I* would have given you.'

'In what way?'

'Doormats, one and all.'

Vittorio leaned forward and snatched the pages out of his friend's hands. 'They can't all be doormats?'

Marcello nodded. 'Every last one of them.'

'Apart from Sirena, you mean.'

'Well, apart from her, clearly. Otherwise that's a carefully curated list of "women who won't."'

Vittorio frowned. 'Won't what?'

Marcello shrugged. 'Argue. Object. Have an opinion on anything or speak their own mind.'

Vittorio gazed at the list more enthusiastically. 'Sounds exactly like what I want!'

'Ah, Vittorio,' Marcello said, shaking his head. 'Some of us know that you're not entirely the bad boy Prince that you like to make out. But you're no walkover either. You'd be bored with any one of these before she'd made it halfway down the aisle. By the time she did you would have plucked a woman from the choir who showed a bit more spirit.'

'All right,' said Vittorio, thrusting the papers onto the nearby coffee table. 'What have *you* got for me?'

'Ah,' said Marcello, a man in his moment. 'Three of the best.' He pushed a folder across the table and flipped open the cover to reveal candidate number one. 'Katerina Volvosky. Former ice-skating supremo, now an international rights lawyer working with the UN. She comes with good, if not royal lineage. Her father is a former ambassador to the USA. Her mother is a doctor—a burns specialist.'

Vittorio nodded. She was attractive, and looked intelligent. 'She definitely looks like she wouldn't be afraid to voice an opinion. What makes you think she'd want to get married?'

'She's just been dumped by her long-term boyfriend, she's thirty-five, and her body clock's ticking. She'd have time for an heir and a spare at the very least. I think, given the right inducement, she could be persuaded to marry you.'

'Huh. As if anyone would need an inducement to marry me.'

Marcello snorted. 'You just go right on believing that, Vittorio.' He turned the page. 'Potential bride number two—Emilija Kozciesko, former animal activist turned environmentalist, a woman with a passion for protecting the Mediterranean in particular. Her mother was president of Ursubilia for ten years, her father is a concert pianist who put his career aside to support his wife's political aspirations. And—get this—she speaks eight languages.'

Vittorio looked at the picture. She was beautiful too, but with a feistiness in her features that said she would fight tooth and nail for what she believed in. No doormat there. She was standing on the bow of a boat, looking out to sea, with the wind catching her long hair. Dark hair that reminded him of something. *Someone*. He dug his hand deeper into his pocket.

'And her body clock?'

'No issues. She's twenty-eight, but she's a rebel who recognises that it's easier to agitate when you're attached to a title.'

Vittorio held out one hand. 'Pass me that list of doormats again.'

'Hah!' Marcello said, sweeping them out of reach. 'Be serious. Now, option number three…' He flipped the page to a photograph of a stunning blonde with Nordic good looks. 'Inga Svenson. Shipping heiress whose family has fallen on hard times. Former model, B-grade actress and now children's ambassador. She's also fluent in French, Italian, English…along with all the Scandinavian languages, of course.'

Vittorio was impressed. 'And she hasn't found a husband yet because…?'

'She was engaged to be married when the family business imploded. She got unceremoniously dumped and the fiancé promptly found himself another heiress.' Marcello eyed his friend. 'She's vulnerable, and I know how you like to rescue vulnerable things.'

Vittorio's fingers squeezed tight.

'What's that in your hand?' asked Marcello.

'What?' Vittorio looked down to see Rosa's earring in his fingers. He hadn't even realised he'd been playing with it. 'Oh, just a trinket,' he said, putting it back in his trouser pocket.

Marcello looked at him levelly. 'A trinket that you keep in your pocket? Have you taken to collecting souvenirs, Vittorio? Because if you have that could be a precursor to something entirely more sinister.'

Vittorio snorted and leaned forward in his chair. 'You make me laugh, my friend.'

He lined up the three photographs next to each other and pushed away the middle one—Emilija, with the dark hair that reminded him of someone.

'Right, how do you propose we do this?'

CHAPTER TEN

'ROSA!' CHIARA YELLED, thumping her roommate on the chest with a pillow. 'Get out of bed. You'll be late.'

'Ow, that stung,' Rosa said, rubbing her sore chest as she struggled to come to. Her head felt full, as if it had somehow absorbed her pillow in the night. But Chiara was right—she needed to get up. Rosa was usually the first of the two to get ready, but lately that was changing, and Chiara was already dressed in her uniform and tying her hair back.

Rosa swung her legs over the side of the bed and pushed herself upright—and immediately wished she hadn't. She put her hand to her mouth. Whatever had been on that pizza last night must have disagreed with her.

'God, you look awful,' Chiara said, watching her. 'What's wrong with you?'

'I don't feel—'

She didn't get any further. A wave of heat welled up inside her and Rosa bolted for their tiny bathroom, where she collapsed boneless while her stomach rebelled against the world.

'You really are sick,' said Chiara, handing her

a wet hand towel once the heaving spasms had passed, leaving Rosa breathless and almost too weak to wipe her heated face.

'Must have been the pizza,' Rosa said, gasping, pressing her face into the towel.

'We shared the pizza. It can't be that.'

'You feel okay?'

'I'm fine. And I had all the wine, because you said you didn't like how it smelt, so if anyone should feel sick it's me.'

'So if it wasn't that pizza, and it couldn't have been the wine, what else can it be?' Rosa struggled to her feet and splashed more cold water on the towel, wiped her neck and throat. 'Please let it not be the flu. I can't afford to take time off.'

She put her hands on the sink and leaned against them, waiting for her body to calm. She took a breath and looked up, and caught sight of her roommate's scowling expression in the mirror over the sink.

'What?'

'You felt queasy yesterday at breakfast too.'

She shook her head, pushing herself away from the sink. She really needed to get moving. 'The coffee was too strong. I felt fine all day after that.'

'You love your coffee.'

Not yesterday, Rosa hadn't. One whiff and she'd turned her head away.

She threw off her nightgown and pulled her

uniform from the hanger on the single clothes rail the girls shared. 'An aberration,' she said.

Chiara watched her clamber into the button-up dress. 'Only…if you think about it…it's about six weeks since Carnevale.'

'So?' Rosa looked around. 'Where are my shoes? Have you seen my shoes?' she asked, only to see the heels poking out from under her bed, where she always left them.

'Six weeks since you got lost and said you met someone. A man…' She let that sink in before she asked, 'When was your last period, Rosa?'

Rosa lifted her head, her expression deadpan as she thought back, counting the weeks, finding they didn't add up. 'Come on, Chiara. Now you're frightening me.'

'Aha!' Chiara said. 'And why would you be frightened? Unless there's something you're not telling me.'

'Stop it,' she said, pushing past her to go back into the bathroom.

She looked at her face in the mirror. She needed to slap on some make-up and do something to fix the weird pallor of her skin…hide the dark shadows under her eyes. She couldn't be pregnant. She just couldn't.

'You had sex with him, didn't you?' Chiara said. 'This stranger who took you to a party.'

'You make it sound shabby,' Rosa protested. 'It wasn't like that.'

'Aha! Then you *did* sleep with him!'

'Okay, so I did. What of it?'

Chiara clapped her hands, her eyes alight at the admission. 'And you never said a word.'

'I don't know why you're so excited,' Rosa said.

'Sorry,' Chiara said, looking suitably penitent. 'I'm just happy for you. Was it good?'

'Chiara!'

'All right. All right. But you could be pregnant, then?'

'I can't be pregnant.' She fiddled in her make-up bag, searching. She was absolutely ruling out being pregnant. 'He used contraception.'

'Condoms aren't one hundred per cent reliable,' Chiara said. 'And you're not on the pill, are you?'

'Of course I'm not!'

Chiara rolled her eyes, but had the good sense not to say anything about that. 'Do your breasts feel tender?'

Rosa's hand stalled on the mascara wand that she'd just started wielding over her lashes. She flicked her eyes to Chiara's, remembering the pillow she'd been walloped in the chest with. *How did she know?*

'Maybe it's just a twenty-four-hour bug? I don't know. But until I know for sure I'm not going to panic about it.'

Like hell. Just the thought of being pregnant made her feel sick with fear.

'I'll get a test from the pharmacy at lunch,' Chiara offered. 'You need to do it as soon as you can.'

Rosa shook her head. 'Don't waste your money.' *Please, God, let it be a waste of money.* 'Anyway, if anyone is going to be buying a test it should be me.'

'No. You'll put it off because you don't want to know, just in case you are. But you need to know one way or the other, and the sooner the better. Because if you are pregnant you need to start thinking about your options.' Then her roommate smiled and gave her a quick hug. 'Now, are you sure you're feeling well enough to go to work?'

The only good thing about that morning was that an entire tour group had checked out and the hotel was down two cleaners who had the flu. She didn't have time to panic, she told herself, exhausted after the third room-clean and change-over. She operated on autopilot, not letting herself think about anything beyond linen and towels and scooping away all the used bottles of cheap toiletries and replenishing them with new.

Because if she didn't think, she couldn't panic. And if she didn't panic, then she wouldn't work herself up over something that was probably nothing.

Though why would her period be late…?

Stress. Overwork. Money worries. That would probably do it. It wasn't as if she was in denial… she was just considering the other options. Making sense of it.

By the time her lunch break rolled around Rosa wanted to tell Chiara to forget it. She was feeling much better than she had in the morning. But Chiara had already slipped away to the *farmacia* and was having none of it.

She tugged Rosa into their tiny basement flat and then their tiny bathroom, passed her the box, and said, 'Do it.'

Rosa looked at the packet, read the instructions. 'It says to do it first thing in the morning.'

'Rosa,' her friend growled, pointing at the toilet behind her shoulder. 'Go.'

She did as she was ordered this time, but she grumbled all the way from the opening of the box, through the peeing on the stick to the waiting.

There was no point. She couldn't be pregnant. It was a waste of money and she'd be delighted to tell Chiara when the test showed up as negative.

Except it didn't.

She swallowed. Looked at the instructions again in case she'd read them wrongly. Looked back at the stick. She had never been more grateful that she was sitting down.

Chiara banged on the door. 'Well, what's happening? What does it say?'

Rosa washed her hands, splashing a little water on her face for good measure. She lifted her heated face to the mirror. She didn't look any different. A little paler than usual, maybe, and her eyes a little wide with shell shock.

She didn't *feel* any different. Shouldn't she feel different? Shouldn't she know? But pregnant… A baby… She was going to be a mother.

Rosa swallowed and looked down at the hand she'd curled low over her abdomen. And she realised the price for one night of sin wasn't just the loss of one of her grandmother's earrings.

The price was much, much higher.

'Come on!' cried Chiara impatiently from outside the door. 'What's going on?'

Rosa took a deep breath and opened the door, holding up the stick. 'Apparently I'm pregnant.'

And she let Chiara's arms enfold her.

'But if I'm pregnant,' Rosa said, sitting on her bed and nursing the cup of sweet tea that Chiara had made for her. 'Doesn't Vittorio have a right to know? Don't I have a responsibility to tell him?'

'There's no "if" about it. You're pregnant,' Chiara said. 'And why do you think he'd want to know?'

'Because he's the father?'

'Have you seen this man since?'

'No. Not since that night.'

'Did he give you his phone number? Anything else so you could contact him?'

'No. Only his first name.' Rosa shook her head. 'He said it was only for one night.'

Chiara sat back and slapped her hands on her legs. 'That says it all, right there. He's married.'

'No!'

'Face it, Rosa. A man picks you up and makes love to you and tells you that it's one night only— what do you *think* that means? His wife is probably about to give birth to their fourth *bambino* and didn't feel like going out that night. Do you really think he'll want to know he's got another one on the way?'

'No. He's not like that!'

'How do you know? You knew him for all of ten minutes, and that was most likely spent with him working out the fastest way to get inside your pants.'

'Stop it! It wasn't like that!'

'All right. But seeing as you haven't told me what it *was* like, what am I supposed to think?'

Rosa flicked her eyes up to her friend. 'Vittorio said his father wants him to get married.' Hadn't that been why Sirena was pursuing him? So that she would be the next Mrs... Mrs... She

didn't know what. He'd never told her what his surname was.

She swallowed. So that she couldn't find him?

'Right. And he does what his father tells him, does he? How old was he? Twelve?'

'Chiara!'

'Well, who does what their father demands when they're all grown up?'

'So he has a demanding father? I don't know.'

Chiara gave an exasperated sigh. 'Clearly.' Then she sat down next to Rosa on the bed and put an arm around her shoulders. 'But you know, you might as well forget about him. You've got more pressing things to worry about now.' She gave her shoulders a squeeze. 'Like what you're going to do about this pregnancy.'

'What do you mean, what I'm going to do about it? I'm pregnant, aren't I? What *can* I do?'

'Oh, *cara*,' her roommate said softly. 'You must know it's not the only way you have to go. There are things you can do. You don't need a child now—how are you going to provide for it?'

'But it's a *baby*, Chiara. I'm having a baby.'

'It's not *technically* a baby yet, though, is it?'

'But it will grow.'

'I'm not saying you shouldn't do it, all I'm saying is having the child is not your only option. You need to think about all your options, Rosa, and what is best for you.'

'And the baby?' Rosa sniffed, her hand already wrapped protectively over the belly under which it lay. 'What about what's best for the baby?'

'I can't answer that,' said Chiara, 'but I can honestly say that there are plenty of children living in dreadful circumstances who would probably have preferred not to have been born at all.' She smoothed the hair from Rosa's brow. 'All I'm saying is think about it, okay? Don't assume that you're trapped and that you have no choices. You have choices. They might not be easy, but they're there.'

CHAPTER ELEVEN

'WHAT THE HELL'S wrong with you, Vittorio?' Marcello said. 'You're not taking this seriously. How do you expect to find yourself a bride to marry by the date your father decreed if you won't ask one?'

Vittorio sighed, hands in pockets, and turned away from the big windows overlooking the Grand Canal. More than halfway through the three months his father had decreed and he was back in Venice—although the intention had been to bring either Katerina or Inga to Venice with him and formally propose.

It was a business decision first and foremost, sure, but Marcello had suggested that no woman was going to say no in such a romantic setting, even if the wedding itself would have to take place in the cathedral in Andachstein.

The worst of it was that he didn't understand it himself. He'd decided to comply with his father's demands. He'd decided to follow his destiny. He'd decided it was a good thing. Perfect. Failsafe. And yet…

'For God's sake Vittorio, what are you thinking?'

'Nothing.'

Marcello sighed theatrically. 'Tell me something I don't know. Now, let's take this from the top. Katerina Volvosky. What do you think of her?'

'She seems nice,' he conceded. They'd been twice to the opera, and had flown to Paris in the royal jet for dinner one night.

'*Nice,*' said Marcello, deadpan. 'Right. How about Inga?'

Vittorio nodded. Together they'd gone ballooning in Turkey, with a side visit to Petra in Jordan. 'Yes, she's nice too.'

'And you can't decide between these two…' he made apostrophes in the air with his fingers '…*"nice"* women?'

'No,' Vittorio said on a shrug. And they *were* nice women. Lovely women, both. 'There's nothing wrong with either of them,' Vittorio said. 'They'd both be fine.' They were intelligent, passionate about their interests and attractive. 'They'd both be an asset to Andachstein.'

'So let's take it back to basics, shall we? Let's make it really, really easy for you.'

Vittorio turned back to look out at the shifting traffic on the canal, his fingers toying with the earring in his trouser pocket. 'I wish you would.'

Because he wasn't finding any of it easy as his eyes sought out the direction of the hotel where Rosa worked. What would she be doing right

now? Would she be on her lunch break? Did she even *get* a lunch break?

'Which woman is better in bed?'

'What?' Vittorio spun around.

'Which one—Katerina or Inga—do you like better in bed?'

Vittorio's eyebrows shot up, answering the question with another. He shrugged. 'I don't know.'

'They're both as good as each other?'

Vittorio turned back to the view. 'I haven't slept with them.'

Marcello blinked. Slowly. 'You haven't slept with them? *You?*' He pressed the knuckle of one finger into the bridge of his nose. 'Vittorio,' he said, looking up, 'don't mind me asking this, but are you all right? Health-wise, I mean? Is there something you're not telling me?'

Vittorio shook his head. 'Never better.'

Marcello looked as if he didn't believe him. What was his problem? The women were nice enough, certainly, and they'd given him enough cues to let him know that they wouldn't say no if he did ask. It was just that when it came down to it he hadn't felt like taking them to bed.

'Okay,' said a weary-sounding Marcello. 'Then all I can suggest to sort this out is to flip a coin.' He held out his hand. 'Have you got one on you?'

'No,' he said, turning back to the canal and looking in the direction of the Dorsodura *ses-*

tiere, where her hotel was situated. But he did have an earring.

'Is there something out there?' asked Marcello, coming closer to see for himself. 'Something that I'm missing?'

'No,' Vittorio said.

Not something. Someone. He'd always intended to return Rosa's earring and, given that he was back in Venice, there was no time like the present.

Serendipity.

'I have to go,' he said, already heading for the stairs.

'But, Vittorio, you need to make a decision—'

'Later,' he said. *'Ciao.'*

Vittorio strode purposefully through the narrow streets of Venice. He wasn't wearing leather today, nor even a swirling cloak, and yet people still moved out of his way when they saw him coming, flattening themselves against the walls of the *calles* or ducking into shop and café doorways.

He barely noticed. He was a man on a mission and he was too busy working out how long it had been since he'd seen her to care. Carnevale... Six weeks ago? Seven? Did she still work at the same hotel? Was she still in Venice or had she moved on? Or gone home to her tiny village in Puglia?

The sooner he got to the hotel, the sooner he'd find out.

Eventually he found it—a shabby-looking hotel, tucked away in the corner of a square with a tiny canal running down one side. The entire side of the wall looked as if it was leaning into it.

He marched through the entry doors that announced it as Palazzo d'Velatte into a tiny foyer and saw heads swivel towards him. He marched towards a thin man sporting a backwards horseshoe of hair and standing behind a tiny counter. He wouldn't swear on a stack of bibles, but he was sure he saw the man swallow.

'Are you checking in?' he asked, craning his neck so high there was no missing the Adam's apple in his throat, bobbing up and down.

'No. I'm looking for someone who works here. A woman.'

'Erm...' The man offered a simpering smile. 'We don't offer that kind of service.'

'She's a cleaner. Her name is Rosa. Does she still work here?'

'I'm not sure I can divulge that—'

Vittorio leaned over the reception desk. 'Does. She. Still. Work. Here?'

The man's eyes bugged. 'Well, yes, but...' His eyes darted to his watch. 'She won't finish her shift for another two hours.'

'So she's working today? In this hotel?'

'Well, yes...'

Vittorio smiled—although it was probably

more of a baring of his teeth, because he noticed he didn't get one in return. 'Then I'll find her myself.'

He looked around the tiny foyer, spied a likely set of stairs and set off.

'Wait!' the man called. 'You can't do that.'

'Watch me,' he said, taking the steps three at a time.

There were only three levels. It shouldn't take long.

On the first level he found nothing.

On the second level he found a cleaner backing out of a room and towing a vacuum cleaner behind her.

'Rosa?' he asked.

The woman looked up. She was a pretty woman, with bright eyes and dark curly hair tied back in a ponytail behind her head, but definitely not Rosa.

Her eyes narrowed when she saw him. She straightened, looking him up and down, frankly assessing. 'You're looking for Rosa?'

'Do you know where I can find her?'

'Your name wouldn't be Vittorio, by any chance?'

'What if it is?' he said.

Her eyes widened in appreciation before they flicked upwards. 'In that case, she's working the floor above.'

* * *

It was the worst day of her life. She'd started the morning throwing up and now, after confronting the room of some guests who had clearly thought last night was party night, only to lose the 'party' they'd consumed all over the bathroom, she kept right on heaving while she cleaned up the mess and cleared away the soiled towels. They were empty retches, because there was nothing in her stomach to bring up, but that didn't stop her retching all the same.

But she could hardly beg off work, because she needed this job and she didn't need anyone knowing she was pregnant. Not until she'd worked out what to do.

Dio, she felt so drained.

She replaced all the towels in the now clean bathroom with fresh ones and then caught sight of her reflection in the bathroom mirror as she swung around. She was shocked at what she saw. She looked like a ghost of herself. Her dull, lifeless eyes were too big for her head, and her hair stuck together in tendrils around her face after her temperature had spiked during each pointless yet violent round of dry heaving.

She needed to take a moment to get herself straightened up before anyone saw her like this.

'Rosa!' someone called in a booming deep

voice, and a shudder went down her spine and sent the muscles clenching between her thighs.

She knew that voice. She'd heard it in her dreams at night. She'd imagined hearing it a hundred times a day in the crowded *calles* and the market stalls along the busy canals. She'd looked around, searching for the source, but it had never been him, of course.

'Rosa!' she heard—even closer.

Her heart thudded loudly in her chest. She wasn't imagining it this time. She peeked out of the bathroom to see a bear of a man entering the room. So tall and broad, with his mane of hair brushed back from his face, his carved features fixed into a frown.

'Vittorio…' she whispered, before her insides twisted on a rush of heat and sent her lurching once more for the pan.

There was nothing to lose. Nothing to give up but the strength in her bones and any shred of self-respect she'd ever had as she gagged where she'd flopped, huddled on the floor. But for him to see her this way was beyond cruel.

And yet he was by her side in an instant, pressing a damp towel to her heated forehead, his big hand on her back, as if lending her strength. As if he were saying, *I'm here*.

Gradually the churning eased, the spasms passed. She had the strength to lean back, to take the dampened towel from his hands and press it to her face. *Dio*, how could she let him see her ghastly face?

'What are you doing here?' she said, between gasps.

'What's wrong with you?' he replied, ignoring her question. 'You're ill.'

'No,' she said, trying to struggle to her feet.

She was confused. She still had rooms to clean, and Vittorio was here, and she didn't understand any of it.

When she turned, Chiara was there at the door to the room, silently watching.

'Are you going to tell him?' she said.

'Tell me what?' he said, looking from one woman to the other, but she could see by the dawning realisation on his face that he was already working it out for himself.

She looked up into a face that spoke of power and strength and everything she lacked in this moment, and told him. 'I'm so sorry, Vittorio, but I'm pregnant.'

He roared. A cry of anguish or triumph she couldn't be sure. But before she could decide she was swept up into his strong arms and cradled against his chest. She could have protested. She was hardly an invalid. She could walk. But instead of protesting she simply breathed him in, The scent was as she remembered. Masculine.

Evocative. It was all she could do not to melt into the *whump-thump* of his heart in his chest.

'Where is her room?' she heard him say.

Followed by Chiara's voice. 'I'll show you.'

'I have to finish my shift,' she said weakly.

'No, you don't.'

He laid her down on her bed. Reverently. Gently. As if she were a fragile piece of glass blown by a master craftsman rather than made of flesh and blood.

'Leave us,' he told Chiara, and the usually bossy but now boggle-eyed Chiara didn't bother trying to argue with him and meekly withdrew.

He sat down beside her and smoothed the damp hair from Rosa's brow. 'It's mine?' he asked.

'What do you think?' she snapped, through a throat that felt raw from throwing up.

He smiled at that, although she didn't understand why. There was nothing funny that she could see about any of this.

He looked around at the tiny windowless room that contained two beds—cots, really—a small chest of drawers that doubled as a bedside table with a lamp between them, and a hanging rack filled with an assortment of clothes.

'This is where you live?'

She nodded, her strength returning enough that

she could scoot herself upright with her back to the wall. 'With Chiara.'

'The two of you?' he asked, clearly aghast. 'Here? Barely above the water level?'

'It's not that bad. It's cheap for Venice. Chiara said it only floods at king tides, and not very often.'

He shook his head and swore softly under his breath. 'Have you seen a doctor?'

'Not yet,' she said. 'I was still—'

'Working out what to do about it?'

He'd stiffened as he said it and she noticed an edge to his voice. A harsh edge. Judgmental?

She swallowed. 'I was still coming to terms with it. I only found out a couple of days ago.'

He pulled out his phone, thumbing through it. 'When were you going to tell me?'

Rosa closed her eyes. Maybe this was another of her dreams. Maybe the hormones running through her bloodstream had turned her a little bit mad and she'd conjured Vittorio up—a combination of thin air and wishful thinking.

'Well?'

She opened her eyes, half surprised that he was still there. 'Chiara said you wouldn't want to know. That you probably had a wife and four *bambini* tucked away somewhere.'

'Why would you believe that when you were there that night? You heard what Sirena said. You knew my father wanted me to marry her. Why listen to Chiara?'

'Because you told me "one night and one night only." That you didn't do for ever. It made as much sense as your father wanting you to marry his friend's daughter.'

This time he swore out loud.

'You mean you *don't* have a wife and children somewhere?'

He smiled down at her, and then whoever he was calling picked up. 'Elena, I need some help,' he said, and issued a list of demands. 'We're going to get you seen to,' he said. 'My housekeeper is organising it. She knows everyone in Venice. And meanwhile we're going out.'

She shook her head. 'I should get back to work. I've been away too long already.'

'You're not going back to work today. If I have anything to do with it you're never going to clean another room in your life.'

'What?'

'Are you all right to walk now?'

She nodded. She felt a million times stronger than she had before, but she was still confused. Nothing he said made sense. The fact he was even here made no sense.

'Good. Then get changed,' he said, gently pressing his lips to her forehead. 'I'm taking you out.'

'Where to?'

'First of all I'm taking you somewhere you can get a decent meal. You need feeding up. And then we're going to sit down for a talk.'

He took her to a restaurant tucked away in an alleyway behind the Rialto Bridge, where the tables were dressed in red and white checked tablecloths. Clearly they were off the tourist trail, in a restaurant that catered to locals, because instead of the multitude of languages she was used to hearing in the hotel and the *calles* the predominant language was Italian.

There they lunched on the best *spaghetti alle vongole* Rosa had ever tasted—but then, she wasn't just hungry by then, she was ravenous. The pasta with tiny clams filled a void inside her, and her once rebellious stomach welcomed every mouthful. Relished it.

Not even the presence of this man opposite could stop her. He seemed to heighten her appetite along with her senses. Maybe it was because he was content just to eat his own pasta as he watched her eat hers, watching approvingly every mouthful she consumed.

But there was something going on behind those cobalt blue eyes, she could see. Something that went beyond ensuring that she ate well. Something calculating. Unnerving.

'What have you been doing the last few weeks?'

she asked between mouthfuls, wanting to break the tension, to see if she could encourage him to say what was on his mind.

'This and that,' he said, giving nothing away. 'What about you?'

'Same. Work, mostly. I was planning to take a few days off and go home. Rudi, one of my brothers, and his wife Estella are due to welcome their second child soon. But that was before I found out—well, you know.'

'Why wouldn't you still go home?'

She shook her head, halting her loaded fork halfway between bowl and mouth. 'I don't know that I can face my father or my family right now. I don't think my head's in the right place.'

'Will they even be able to tell so early?'

'It's not that. It's because I feel like I've let them down. Papà wanted me to live and see the world—he wouldn't have encouraged me to leave the village otherwise. But I don't think he was expecting this to happen. Not to me. Not so soon.'

'Would he be angry?'

'No. Not exactly. Probably just—disappointed.' She put her fork down and looked up at him. 'And isn't that worse?'

Vittorio didn't know. He had a father who specialised in anger. He'd got so used to disappointing his father over the years it was no longer a deterrent. If it ever had been. It had become more like a blood sport between them rather than a familial relationship.

Rosa finished off the last of her pasta and leaned back in her seat. 'That was amazing. Thank you.'

'Good,' he said. 'And now we need to talk.'

'I'm ready,' she said.

But he shook his head, looking at the tables full of diners clustered around them—tables full of diners who all spoke Italian and who might overhear. 'Not here.'

She had to hand it to Vittorio—if you had to sit down to have a talk you could find a worse venue than floating down the Grand Canal. She'd raised her eyebrows when he'd stopped at the gondola stand, but he'd merely shrugged and said, 'When in Venice...' and handed her into the gently rocking vessel.

He was doing it again—sweeping her out of her world and into his—but this time there was no panic. No fear. Because it was broad daylight and she knew enough about him to trust him. Besides, it was his child that she carried in her womb. His seed that had taken root.

Once they were seated on the golden bench the gondolier set off, sweeping his oar rhythmically behind them in the time-honoured way, sending the long, sleek vessel effortlessly skimming over the surface of the canal.

All these months she'd been in Venice and never once had she taken a gondola ride. It was something for the tourists, and hideously expensive in her eyes, but here on the water you gained a different perspective. It was seeing Venice as it was meant to be seen, from the watery streets that made up its roadmap.

For a while they were content to take in the views and point out the sights as they slid under the magnificent white Rialto Bridge, with its eleven arches, crowded with tourists looking down at the passing traffic, looking down at them with envy.

And if Venice in the fog had been atmospheric and mystical, under the pale blue skies of spring it turned magical. It was as if the city had been re-born and emerged fresh and renewed from under its winter coat.

The colours of the buildings popped. Red brickwork stained with salt, pastel pink and terracotta, Tuscan yellows and even shades of blue trimmed with white competed for attention as they stood shoulder to shoulder above the slick green-grey waters of the canal.

And at its heart were the waterways they traversed, the canals alive with *vaporetto* and motorboats and gondolas all fighting for space. For a few minutes they were just two more tourists, enjoying the sights and sounds.

And there, with Vittorio smiling at her, she couldn't imagine a place she'd rather be—not even at home in her village, with her *papà* and her brothers and their families nearby. It was magical. And the most magical thing about it was that Vittorio was actually here, bursting into her life as suddenly as he had on that cold, fog-bound night of Carnevale.

It was no wonder that she'd missed him. No wonder that she'd dreamed of him. He was tall and broad and powerful. He was larger than life. He was—*more*. More than anything she'd ever experienced before. And he made her feel more alive than she'd ever felt.

At one stage she was smiling up at the bridge they were about to pass under when she turned and saw the he was taking a photograph of her. She tried to protest. 'I would have made more of an effort,' she said, pulling her hair away from her face.

'You look beautiful,' he said, and her heart felt as if it would bursting.

And still the question that he had not yet answered hung between them.

'Why did you come today?' she asked. 'I never expected to see you again.'

'I came with one purpose. But now you have given me another.'

Her brow furrowed with confusion. 'I don't understand…'

He took her hand in his. 'I wanted to see you, even if briefly. And seeing you again has reminded me. We were good together, Rosa.'

Sensation skittered down her spine. She blinked. She hadn't known what to expect, but certainly not that. 'It's good to see you.'

More than good. She'd dreamed about him. Had replayed every moment of their lovemaking until she could run it on a loop in her head, and the experience was still as exciting as it had been the first time.

He smiled as he pressed her hand to his lips. 'What are you going to do?'

Back to that. She looked at the buildings, glorious relics of centuries gone by and still defying the logic that said buildings must be built on solid ground.

She turned back to him. 'What can I do? I have so few options. But I want to do what's best for the baby.'

He nodded and squeezed the hand he still held.

'Marry me.'

The words were gone before she could grasp and process them, lost on the lapping waters and the hustle and bustle and sounds of the busy canal. She couldn't have heard right.

'*Scuzi?*'

'Marry me. Our child will have a mother and a father and you'll have no need to feel ashamed when you go home. And you'll never have to clean another hotel bathroom in your life.'

She laughed. 'Don't be ridiculous, Vittorio. I don't expect a proposal. That's crazy.'

'Rosa, I mean it.'

She looked up into his face and the fervent look in his blue, blue eyes stopped her in her tracks. 'You're actually serious?'

'Of course I'm serious.'

'But it's so sudden. You can't make a decision like that so quickly.'

'I already have.'

'But *I* can't!'

The idea was ridiculous. There were all kinds of reasons why it made no sense. They barely knew each other. And it was so early in her pregnancy—anything could happen, and then they'd be stuck together, and one or both of them would resent it for ever.

The gondola slipped slowly down the sinuous canal and the richly decorated *palazzos* drifted by, at odds with the turmoil going on in Rosa's mind.

She'd always wanted to marry for love. She wanted what her mother and father had shared before her mother had been cruelly wrenched from them by her disease: a deep, abiding love, the kind of love that took death to break it apart.

She knew that it was no idle dream, no fantasy that she aspired to, that she wished for herself. She'd witnessed it first-hand, initially with her grandparents and then with her parents, and she wanted it for herself. More than that, she believed she deserved it.

So this—Vittorio's bizarre offer—wasn't how it was supposed to be. This was all wrong. She was pregnant by a man she'd met only once before and now he was asking her to marry him because of the baby she was carrying.

It was so not how she'd imagined a proposal to be.

It would be crazy to say yes.

Even if a part of her was tempted.

She gasped in a breath as she numbly watched the passing parade. How many nights had she lain awake, when all was silent aside from Chiara's soft breathing, and thought about that night? Replaying the events, the emotions, the heart-stopping pleasures of the flesh he'd revealed to her? He'd taught her so much. Had given her so much.

For how many nights had she dreamed he would come for her?

And here he was.

And if a city could defy logic and be built atop the sea then maybe what he said could make some kind of sense too. He'd come for her today. Despite saying they'd never see each other again.

He'd tilted her world off its axis in just one night. If he could do that, then maybe it wasn't so impossible. Maybe they had what it took to make a marriage work?

She turned back to him. 'Did you come here today to ask me to marry you?' she asked.

'No,' he said, slipping his hand into his trouser pocket. 'Otherwise I would have come prepared with a ring to offer you. But I do have this…'

And there, in the palm of his hand, lay her grandmother's gold and pearl earring.

Her hand went to her mouth as her heart skipped a beat. She could scarcely believe it. She reached down to touch it, still not believing it was real, curling her fingers around the precious item, still warm from being tucked away next to Vittorio's body.

'This is the reason I came today. I found it nestled on your pillow after you had gone.'

She looked up at him. 'But I went to your *palazzo*. Your housekeeper said nothing had been found.'

'She didn't know. I intended to return it before now.'

'I thought I'd lost it for ever.'

'I meant to have Elena package it up and send it to you. But then, if I had…'

She looked up at him as electricity zipped

down her spine. 'You might never have found out about the baby.'

He smiled down at her. 'Serendipity,' he said.

And she curled the hand holding the earring close to her chest, tears of gratitude, of relief, of joy, pricking at her eyes.

'Or maybe fate, or even destiny.'

Or magic, she thought as he pulled her into his kiss. *Don't forget magic.*

It was like coming home, her lips meeting his, their warm breath intermingling, the taste of him in her mouth. And she wondered if a day that had started so badly, so desolate and without hope, could get any better.

He drew back as the gondolier drew his vessel into a private dock outside a *palazzo*. And even though it had been foggy the one night he'd brought her here she would have recognised it in a heartbeat.

Vittorio's *palazzo*.

He was on his feet and had leapt onto the deck like a natural before he handed her out of the vessel. He slipped the gondolier some notes and then collected her arm to lead her inside.

'There's one more thing I need to tell you. One more reason you need to agree to marry me.'

CHAPTER TWELVE

'Now I *KNOW* this is some kind of joke.' Rosa burst from the chair she'd been settled in, needing to pace the room in long, frantic strides. 'You can't do this to me, Vittorio. You can't ask me to marry you—can't try to convince me to marry you with your kisses and your sweet talking about destiny and fate—and then drop a bombshell by telling me you're a prince. The Prince of Andachstein, no less!'

'Rosa, calm down.'

'How do you expect me to calm down? How did you think I'd react? That I would bow and scrape and be grateful that I've been offered this royal condescension? Am I supposed to be humbled? Or intimidated? Or both?'

'Rosa, listen!'

'No. I don't want to listen. I'm going home.'

She turned towards the doors—gilt-framed doors, elaborately carved with tigers and elephants, just one more treasure in a *palazzo* dripping with treasures of Murano glass and crystal chandeliers and rich velvet-upholstered antiques.

And it wasn't as if she hadn't noticed the insane luxury of this *palazzo* before. How had she

accepted his explanation that it was simply somewhere he stayed without realising that he must
have connections to the rich and famous—or that
he must be one of them? Had she been so blinded
by lust at that stage that she hadn't cared to notice? That she hadn't been able to see what was
in front of her face?

She sniffed. 'Don't bother showing me out. I
found the way myself once before. I can find my
way home.'

'What? Home to your squalid basement apartment and your hand-to-mouth cleaning job?
Home to throwing up every morning while you
clean up somebody else's mess? Why would you
want to go back to that life when I can offer you
so much more?'

She spun on her heel. 'Because it's *my* life,
Vittorio,' she said, her hands over her chest. 'It
might be hard, and it might involve cleaning up
the filth and garbage of other peoples' lives, but
it's the life I choose to lead because that's the life
I know. That's the world I belong to—not yours.'

'And you think, therefore, that that's the only
life you deserve? You sell yourself short, Rosa. I
would never have expected that.'

'I thought you belonged to my world too. At
least that you were closer to my world. When
you took me to the party that night you made me
think that you were on the fringes of Marcello's

world. "He's descended from the *doges* of Venice," you told me. I asked you how you knew such people. "Friends," you said. Your father and his were friends. Just friends. You let me think your father worked for him, and yet your father sits on the throne of Andachstein. Were you laughing at me when I told you I understood? When I told you about my father working for the mayor of our small village? Because you should have been. You sure made a fool out of me.'

'No! You constructed your own story. You believed what you wanted to believe.'

'You could have told me then how wrong I was. But you didn't make one effort to correct me.'

'How was I supposed to tell you? If I'd told you I was a prince in that square would you have believed me? Would you have come with me?'

'Of course not!'

'You see?'

'No! You could have told me you were a prince when we were in the garden before the party.'

'And would you have believed me then?'

She wavered. *Probably not*. But still... 'Look, we slept together. But you can't be serious. You can't expect me to marry you.'

'Rosa,' he said, 'what are afraid of?'

'I'm not afraid.'

'Aren't you? Weren't you ready to say yes to me before, when you thought I was just a man?'

'Well, maybe…'

'Then what's changed? Unless you're afraid that you're not good enough to be a princess? Is that what you're telling me? That you don't deserve it?'

'You should have told me.'

'Did you tell me you were a virgin? Before you were in my bedroom, having already agreed to make love?'

'Maybe not—but it's not like that puts us on an even footing. After all, you're *still* a prince.'

He didn't need her to spell it out. What he needed was for her to agree to marry him.

'Why are you so angry with me? You wanted me to make love to you that night.'

'Yes. I wanted you to make love to me. *You.* Vittorio. The man I met that night. Not the Prince of some random principality I've barely heard of. I wasn't there for *him.*'

'Does it matter? I'm still the same person.'

'Of course it matters! You're next in line to the throne of Andachstein. Royalty. I'm a girl from a tiny village in the heel of Italy. Don't you think there's something of a power imbalance there?'

'I do. But there's another one that we have to deal with. Because you're the one who holds all the cards.'

'I don't see how. Like I said, you're still a prince, whatever I decide.'

'But you're the one carrying the heir.'

She blinked. 'But if we don't—if I don't—'

'There's no escaping it,' he said. 'You can't just sidestep being the mother to the heir of a throne.'

She kicked up her chin. 'It might be a girl. Surely a girl can't be the heir to the throne in a principality steeped in antiquity? Surely the throne can't go to an accidental princess?'

'That's why I'm taking you to a clinic, so that we can find out.' He looked at his watch. 'It's time we were leaving.'

'I didn't say I was going to marry you even if it is a boy.'

'And you didn't rule it out. Let's go.'

'But it's too early to tell,' she said.

'No,' he said. 'It's not.

Rosa could scarcely believe it—that a blood test that took only a few moments could deliver them the sex of their unborn child at such an early stage. But the doctor taking the sample of her blood had assured her it was correct.

'This test is not commercially available yet, but it is accurate in determining the sex of an unborn baby with up to ninety-five percent certainty.'

'What if it's one of the five per cent?' she said while they sat quietly together afterwards. 'What if it is a girl?'

'I'll take that risk. Meanwhile, you carry my

son and the heir to the throne of Andachstein. You can say no to marrying me. You can walk away from this marriage if you choose. But in doing so, know that you are denying our child his rightful destiny.'

'You would put that load on my shoulders?'

'The load is already there. It is up to you what you decide to do with it.'

She turned away, her mind reeling. The pregnancy. The arrival of Vittorio. Finding out he was a prince. A proposal of marriage.

It was like being bombarded from every side with no respite. There was no time to take anything in. No time to process anything. And yet she had to make a decision that would impact her entire life—and that of their unborn child.

She swallowed. 'And if I agree to marry you?'

'Then our son will be brought up to assume his rightful place in Andachstein, with all the rights, privileges and responsibilities that go with it.'

She thought about the tiny basement flat that would never do to bring up a child in. She thought about her home in Zecce, a tiny dot of a dusty village in Puglia, where their child would grow up happy—she would make sure of that—but in no way in wealth or the lap of luxury. And she thought about this *palazzo* that would be part of his heritage, and no doubt much more besides.

Would it be fair to deprive their son of all that

because his father had neglected to inform her that he was a prince?

And the biggest question of them all. What about love? Where did love factor in? He'd said nothing of love.

'What about love?' she asked, her throat so dry she had to force the words out.

'We'll both love our son,' he said.

She squeezed her eyes shut. So that was how it was. She'd read far too much into his sudden arrival, his kind attention, his comfort and his care. She'd read far too much into a romantic gondola ride and the fact that he'd wanted to see her again to return her grandmother's earring, as if it meant something.

But it had been an accident that he'd turned up. A twist of fate. He hadn't come for her at all—he was simply returning a piece of jewellery. And now the only reason he wanted her to stay was because she was having his baby. The child of a prince.

'You're using me,' she said.

'No.'

'Yes! You used me before and now you're using me again. But this time because I'm carrying your child.'

'It's not like that.'

'Isn't it? Then what would you call it? Blackmail? A world of spun gold for my child if I agree to marry you? Otherwise he lives the life of a peasant?'

'Think of the child. It's the best thing for the child. The fair thing.'

She spun away. She didn't want to hear it. Because part of her knew he was right. How could she say no and deprive their child of its birthright?

But this was not how her dreams had looked. Vittorio had come for her, yes, but not the way she'd imagined. Not for love. And now her dreams were turned to dust, and her hopes of love with them.

She couldn't help but wonder whether he had loved his first wife. A stab of jealousy pierced her heart. Or perhaps this was just how royal families did things—even in the twenty-first century— cold, loveless, contractual marriages.

How could she live without love? It was the foundation stone of her very existence. But then, how could she live without Vittorio? Without his touch? With just her dreams to sustain her, to mock her, when she could have the real thing even in the absence of love.

How could she wake up from those dreams to a sense of devastating loss and know that things could have been different if only she hadn't been so headstrong? So proud?

'Think of the child,' he'd said.

And she was. But she was thinking about herself too. Thinking about parting from this man one last time after he'd found her again, and how much harder this time would be when it didn't have to be this way.

In the end, when it came down to it, he wasn't offering her a choice at all.

'All right,' she whispered, feeling her life spiralling out of control. 'I'll marry you.'

But not without conditions.

CHAPTER THIRTEEN

MARCELLO ANSWERED VITTORIO'S call on the third ring. 'I was wondering when I was going to hear from you again,' Marcello said. 'Have you come to your senses and made a decision yet?'

'You'll be delighted to know I have.'

'So who's the lucky lady? Katerina or Inga?'

'Neither.'

'What kind of game are you playing now?' Marcello sounded as if he was at the end of his tether. 'You know—'

'I know. I have to marry someone. So I am. I'm marrying Rosa.'

There was a pause at the end of the line. 'You don't mean—the woman from that night at Carnevale? The one you brought to the party?'

'The very same.'

Marcello snorted. 'Well, it's good you've made a decision, but how is your father going to react to that news?'

'It's other news that might just swing it. She's pregnant, Marcello, and—get this—she's having a boy.'

'You sly dog. You've been seeing her, then.

That explains why your heart wasn't seriously in the hunt for a bride.'

'No, I haven't seen her since Carnevale. Not until today.'

'Ah,' said Marcello. 'She must have made quite an impression on you, in that case. I'm beginning to see why you might have been off your game. If you'd told me you were besotted with the woman it would have saved everyone a lot of time and effort.'

Vittorio growled. 'Stop talking rubbish, Marcello!'

'When are you going to tell your father?'

'As soon as Rosa's father agrees to the marriage.'

There was a pause at the end of the line. 'You—Prince Vittorio of Andachstein—are going to ask a woman's father for permission to marry her? After you've already taken certain liberties with his daughter, evidenced by the fact that she's pregnant with your child?'

Vittorio wished his friend wouldn't make such a big deal out of every single thing. 'Rosa's giving up a lot. She wants to do at least this part the old-fashioned way. We're travelling to Puglia this weekend.'

'And you have agreed?'

'Rosa insisted I meet her family and ask his permission or no wedding.'

'I like this woman more and more,' Marcello declared, chuckling down the phone line. 'I'm so glad to know you're not getting yourself a doormat. But, Vittorio, have you thought about what you're going to do if her father says no?'

'Ciao,' Vittorio said, putting his phone down on the coffee table.

Rosa's father wasn't going to say no. He couldn't.

As for not getting a doormat—he was well aware of that. He'd seen the way she'd stood up to Sirena that night, refusing to be cowed. He'd seen the way she'd stood up to him, insisting that she wasn't going to give up her job and move into the *palazzo* until such time as her father had given permission and the wedding was confirmed to proceed.

He shook his head as he looked around him at the luxurious fittings and furniture of the *palazzo*, all with a view of the Grand Canal. Why she would want to stay in that job and live in her dingy room when she could have all this, he didn't know. But it seemed important to her, and he figured she might as well enjoy what freedom she had now.

Soon enough she would be married to him and she'd find herself bound up in palace protocol and demands that she had no say in. She might as well enjoy her independence now.

He shook his head. No doormat there. With Rosa he was getting the whole package. A woman who could light up his nights, to please him— and who had already proved herself a breeder, to please his father.

What could be better than that?

Unless it was the child. A son.

His son.

It was something he'd yearned for once. Something he'd waited for with every passing month of his marriage. He'd expected it to happen quickly. After all, nothing else had been a problem. He'd been served up a bride he'd fallen madly in love with. All he'd needed was the news that he would become a father and the royal line of Andachstein would live on, his destiny fulfilled.

It had all seemed so easy in those bright, halcyon days. Except his wait had been fruitless. And then he'd discovered the reason why, and his world had turned sour and rancid, with bitterness usurping hope.

This child was like a reclaimed dream. A second chance. But he wouldn't make the same mistake again. He was taking no chances if this marriage didn't work out. He wasn't about to risk losing himself in the process.

There were some places he wouldn't go again. Love was one of them.

CHAPTER FOURTEEN

IT WAS A two-hour drive from Bari Airport to Zucca. First along the straight highway that crossed the ankle of Italy, before turning on to narrower and yet narrower roads that meandered past stone walls and olive groves through the undulating countryside.

The sprinkle of towns and villages here seemed mostly deserted, except for the odd herd of goats and the brightly coloured pots of geraniums and the bougainvillea clambering over crumbling walls. Here and there an old man in a chair outside his house would lift a lazy hand as they passed.

Summer felt closer here, in this far southern region of Italy. The sky was clear blue, the air was clean and warm, and the late April sun held the promise of hot, airless summer days.

Along the route Rosa told Vittorio about her family. There was her father, Roberto, her three brothers, Rudi, Guido and Fabio, and their wives, Estella, Luna and Gabriella. There were three *bambini* between them now, with the addition of Rudi and Estella's second child, born just a week ago. The first granddaughter had been a cause of much excitement, and had been named Maria Rosa after her late grandmother and her aunt.

Vittorio tried to pay attention and take it all in, but it was hard when his gut was roiling. Oddly, he was never afraid to meet his own father, to put up with his disappointment and even his anger, but he was nervous about meeting Roberto. Rosa's father was an unknown quantity, and he suspected that the man wasn't about to be dazzled by his title.

'They're all going to be so excited to learn there's going to be another cousin soon.'

'You don't think it's too early to tell them about the baby?' Vittorio asked.

Rosa wasn't showing yet—not in a way anybody else would notice. Surely only he would appreciate the extra fullness to her breasts and what it meant.

'If we're going to get married because I'm having your baby,' she said, 'why should we pretend otherwise?'

He looked across at her in the passenger seat. There was a strange note to her voice, as if it was fraying around the edges and she was straining to hold it together.

'Are you tired?' he said. They had made an early start to make it to Zucca by lunchtime, and with the flight and then the undulating road he wouldn't be surprised if she was feeling a little motion sick.

'I'm fine,' she said, looking out of her window.

'Is everything all right?'

She sighed, still keeping her head turned away. 'Everything's fine.'

He grunted. Clearly something was wrong, but he wasn't about to argue the point. He'd given her plenty of opportunity to say if anything was bothering her.

They didn't speak for the final ten minutes of their journey, and when they pulled up outside the stone walls of her family home they didn't have to announce their arrival. Their vehicle had obviously been heard, because a swarm of people piled out of the house, their faces beaming, their arms outstretched.

Rosa just about bounded from the car, casting off her strange glumness like a cloak, laughing and squealing as she was gathered into the warm embrace of her family. The realisation that he was somehow the cause of her mood ratcheted up his own grumpiness.

He leaned against the car, his arms crossed, watching the reunion. Such a foreign, unknown thing—like an object he had to study to work out the very shape and texture of it.

So this was family?

Everyone seemed to be speaking at once, voices

piling up one over another, men and women, and the two older babies were being passed around so that Rosa could hug them and cluck over them and remark on how much they'd grown. And there was Rosa, in the midst of the celebrations, hugging and laughing and happy. Everyone was happy.

In the background, with his hands on his hips as he watched on, stood the man who had to be her father. He wasn't as tall as his three sons, but he stood broad-shouldered and rosy-cheeked and proud as he waited for a chance to welcome his daughter home.

'Papà!' he heard her squeal when she saw him, and then they were in each other's arms and everyone was crying and whooping and back-slapping some more.

And then, as if Vittorio were an afterthought, Rosa said something and all heads swivelled towards him. In their gazes he saw interest and suspicion, curiosity and mistrust—until Rosa came back and claimed his hand and pulled him into the fray, introducing him to them all.

It was because he was with her that they welcomed him, he had no doubt. And even if they didn't trust him they welcomed him as Rosa's friend, and not as the heir to the throne of a tiny principality that had been irrelevant to their family until now. He knew who mattered here and it wasn't him, and he felt the power imbalance that she'd pointed out as existing between them tilt markedly the other way.

In Venice she was alone. Vulnerable.

But here she was surrounded by her family, like a guard all around her, and *he* was the outsider, the one who had to prove himself.

They sat down under a vine-covered pergola at a table already spread with platters of antipasto and cheeses and crusty loaves of bread, all sprinkled with dappled light. Rosa handed out gifts for the babies. Gifts she'd made. Sailor suits for the boys and a lacy gown she'd made for the tiny Maria Rosa. Everyone praised Rosa's needlework—gifts she'd made herself on her mother's beloved old sewing machine and all the more special for it.

'Tell us about Andachstein,' Rudi said, pouring ruby-red Puglia wine into glasses.

And Vittorio found himself telling them all about the principality—a gift of the far corner of his lands by an ancient monarch, bestowed upon a knight in return for faithful service. He told them about the *castello*, set high on the hilltop above the sparkling harbour far below. He told them of the landscape, of the rugged wooded hills and the pathways lined with thyme and rosemary that scented the air.

They all listened with rapt attention while they ate and drank wine. Rosa's beautiful eyes were the widest, and she looked both excited and afraid. He realised he'd never spoken to her of the place where she would one day live.

He squeezed her hand to reassure her and the conversation moved on.

The three wives were about to prepare the next course when the sound of a baby crying came from inside the house.

'I'll come and help with lunch,' said Rosa.

'No, you stay,' said Estella, 'I need you here. Wait.'

She was back a few minutes later, dropping a bundle on Rosa's lap. 'Say hello to your auntie Rosa, Maria.'

Rosa's eyes lit up as she took the tiny bundle. 'Oh, Estella, she's beautiful. Look at those big eyes…and such long hair!' The child blinked up at her, her rosebud mouth still moving, tiny hands crossed over her chest.

Vittorio watched as Rosa cradled the child in her arms. Not a two-year-old this time, and not an eleven-month-old like he'd seen her hold before, already halfway to childhood. This was practically a newborn.

And he was struck by the beauty of the tableau.

Something shifted inside him at that moment. It shifted the tiniest of fractions, and yet it was so momentous that for a few moments his throat choked shut.

In a few months Rosa would be holding their child. And if she could look so beautiful, so beatific, holding somebody else's child, how much more rapturous would she look when she was holding theirs?

Everything she did told him that he was doing the right thing. She would be the perfect mother.

'You are so lucky to go to the city and meet your handsome man,' said Luna, generously ladling pasta into bowls that got passed from hand to hand around the table. 'You would never have found anyone as good-looking as Vittorio in the village.'

'Hey,' said Guido, looking aggrieved. 'What's that supposed to mean?'

'Exactly what it sounds like,' said Fabio, rolling his eyes. 'Apparently all the hot guys are in the cities.'

'No,' Rudi said, the voice of authority. 'Luna means all the good men are already taken, don't you, Luna?'

'Is that what you meant, Luna?' laughed Gabriella, clearly not convinced.

Estella laughed too. 'I could have sworn you meant something else entirely.'

'These women,' Rudi said, shaking his head. 'They are something else.' He pointed a finger at their guest in warning. 'Vittorio,' he said, 'don't expect Rosa is going to be any different. And don't, whatever you do, think that she's going to be a pushover. These women, they have a mind of their own.'

'Rudi!' Rosa scolded.

Vittorio just looked sideways at Rosa and smiled. 'I'll keep that in mind.'

Rosa's father wasn't old—not in years anyway— but the creases in his leathered face and the oil stains on his hands spoke of a man who had not just worked but rather had laboured his entire life. A man who had suffered the devastating loss of his wife but who had carried on, welcoming the new generation of Ciavarros one by one.

'Come,' he said to Vittorio after the family had sated themselves on the feast the women had pre- pared. 'We need to have a talk, man to man.'

Rosa squeezed Vittorio's hand as he rose to fol- low Roberto. He was inordinately grateful for the gesture. It was ridiculous, but he hadn't felt this nervous since he was a child, starting boarding school in Switzerland as a seven-year-old, when he'd felt as if he'd gone to a different world, with new languages to grapple with and comprehend, and older boys who'd seen a man-child and de- cided to take him down a peg or two before he was too big and he got the upper hand.

They left the family under the vine-covered pergola and Roberto led him to a patio on the other side of the house via the big kitchen, where he pulled a bottle and two shot glasses from a shelf.

Both men settled themselves down and Roberto poured a hefty slug into each glass, handing Vittorio one.

'To Rosa,' he said, and the pair clinked glasses.

The older man threw his down his gullet. Vittorio followed suit, and felt the liquor set fire to his throat and burn all the way down.

He set his glass on the table without feeling he'd disgraced himself, only to see Rosa's father top the glasses up.

'And to you, Vittorio,' he said, and downed the second glass.

Vittorio swallowed the fiery liquor down, feeling it burst into flames in his belly.

'It's good, no?' said Roberto. 'I make it myself.'

'Very good,' Vittorio agreed, thankful that his voice box still worked.

He was even more thankful to see the stopper placed back in the bottle.

'I hear you want to marry my daughter.'

'I've asked her, it's true.'

'She also tells me that she is carrying your child.'

Vittorio was catapulted right back to school

again—to a summons to the headmaster's office for punching a boy who had been picking on a junior grader. He'd got the *don't think just because you're a prince* speech then, and he half expected to hear it again now.

'Also true.'

The other man nodded and sighed. 'Maria—my wife—was very beautiful. Rosa has her eyes.'

'They're beautiful eyes. The colour of warmed cognac,' Vittorio said.

'Yes,' said Roberto with a wide smile that smacked of approval. 'That's it. I used to tell Maria that I could get drunk just by looking into her eyes.' His eyes brightened. 'She would tell me, "Go and drink your grappa if you want to get drunk. I have work to do."' He laughed a little, then sniffed, ending on a sigh. 'There is a lot of Maria in Rosa. I can promise you, you will never be bored.'

'I know that.'

'But Rosa says that while she wants what's best for the *bambino*, she is not sure.'

His words were like a wet slap about the face.

'It's so sudden,' Vittorio said, 'and there's a lot Rosa will need to take on. It's not a normal marriage, in many respects.'

Roberto nodded. 'True. But then, what *is* a normal marriage? When it comes down to it, every marriage is a game of give and take, of compromise and of bending when one least wants to bend.'

And breaking, Vittorio thought. Sometimes marriages just broke you into pieces.

'Did Rosa tell you I was married once before?'

'*Si,*' he said, with a nod of his head. 'She says you are a widower.'

'It wasn't a good marriage and it didn't end well,' Vittorio said, studying his feet.

'You see,' Roberto said. 'We are not so different. You might be a prince, but we are both widowers, after all. We both know loss.'

'I guess we do,' he said.

'You know,' Roberto said, leaning back in his chair, 'when a man marries a woman for life, and he has a good marriage, and he only gets thirty years, that is nowhere near enough.' He shook his head. 'I am sorry that you haven't found this satisfaction—yet.'

He leaned forward, removing the stopper from the bottle again. He poured two more slugs before he put the stopper back, raised his glass.

'Here is to the marriage of you and Rosa,' he said. 'May it be a good one from the very beginning. And may it be a long one, filled with love.' He nodded, and said, 'I give you my blessing,' before downing the shot.

The liquor stuck in Vittorio's throat and burned.

Or maybe it was her father's words as he'd blessed the union.

Love...

All Vittorio wanted from this marriage was the heir Rosa was carrying. A spare would guarantee the principality's survival. Having Rosa in his bed would be a bonus.

But love?

Surely her father could see that this was a convenient marriage? That love didn't factor into it? Surely he wasn't that unworldly?

But what was he to say in the face of the man's reminiscences about his own loving marriage and his wishes for them to be happy? He could hardly tell Roberto that he would never let himself love his daughter, not when he had been embraced so warmly into the family. That was between him and Rosa.

The man had given his approval. Vittorio swallowed down on the burning in his throat. It didn't feel altogether comfortable, but wasn't Roberto's blessing the thing he'd come for?

The announcement was made. Roberto had given his blessing and the entire family would go to Andachstein for the wedding. Cheers ensued, but a ruddy-cheeked Roberto quelled them, because he had even more news to share—the secret Rosa had shared with him—that in a few months they would be welcoming a new baby into the family, his new grandson.

Bottles of Prosecco appeared from nowhere and corks popped. Toasts were made, backs were slapped, cheeks were kissed, and Vittorio found himself hugged by everybody, men and women, multiple times. His acceptance into the family was now beyond dispute.

The one person who didn't seem to want to hug him was the one he wanted to the most. Rosa had let him quickly kiss her on the lips as everyone had toasted the couple, before she'd swooped upon one of her nephews and sat down, hiding herself beneath him. She knew what she was doing. She was using the child as a human shield. What he didn't understand was why.

He stood in a circle of men and watched her with the child, making a fuss of it, talking with her sisters-in-law and avoiding his eye. It was killing him. It had been so many weeks since he'd taken her to bed that magical night, and having her back in his life, being so close, was an exercise in frustration.

He burned for her. He wanted nothing more than to bury himself in her sweet depths.

But she'd refused to move into the *palazzo* with him. She'd refused to sleep with him. Not until everything was settled, she'd said.

He watched her laughing. Her hair was down

today, curling over her shoulders, dancing in the light spring breeze, and her eyes were warm like cognac heated by a flame.

Well, everything was settled. Her father had given his approval of their marriage. The wedding would go ahead. Andachstein would have its heir.

And tonight he would hold Rosa and make love to her again.

The celebrations were on the wane by late afternoon, and one by one the brothers drifted off to their own homes with their families and sleepy babies. Roberto was sitting in an armchair, quietly snoring, when Rosa said she was tired and was going to turn in.

At last, thought Vittorio.

They collected their overnight bags from the car, and Vittorio felt his anticipation rising with every step back into the house. Rosa was wearing a dress splashed with big bright flowers today, with a full skirt, and a cardigan over her shoulders. He wasn't sure whether he was going to be able to wait to get the dress off before he rucked up her skirt and took her.

'I hope my family wasn't too much for you today,' she said.

'No,' he said as he followed her through the house, his hands itching to hold her, to glide over

her skin, smooth as satin. 'You have a good family. Noisy, but good.'

She laughed a little over her shoulder. 'Definitely noisy.' And then she opened a door. 'Here's where you're sleeping tonight.'

He stepped into the room, confused. He looked around. There was one single bed surrounded by girlie things. A basket of dolls in one corner. Pictures of Rosa growing up. Artwork that she must have done as a child on the walls and a poster of a boy band she must have once followed.

'This is your old room?'

'It's the most comfortable single bed there is. It's yours tonight.'

He tried to pull her into his arms. 'But where are *you* sleeping? I thought that tonight we could celebrate our engagement.'

She laughed again and slipped out of his reach.

'Won't you stay with me?' he invited.

She shook her head. Her beautiful face was lit by a sliver of moonlight through the curtain, and he was reminded of liquid mercury and silver, fluid and impossible to contain.

'I can't make love to you under my father's roof.'

'He's asleep. He won't know.'

'*I'll* know,' she said, shaking her head, smiling softly.

He reached for her again, knowing he could

change her mind if only she would let him kiss her. He knew she would melt in his arms. But she backed off to the door, all quicksilver and evasion.

'Then when?' he said, a cold bucket of resignation pouring down over him. 'When can we make love again?'

'Our wedding night, of course,' she said.

'What? But that's weeks away.' Three or four. Too many to contemplate.

'Then it will be all the more special for waiting.'

'Rosa,' he said, pleading now, raking one hand through his hair.

'No,' she said. 'You're getting what you want. Let me have this.'

'But do you know how long it's been?'

She smiled a sad, soft smile. 'I know how long it's been for me.' She blew him a kiss. 'Goodnight.'

Vittorio was alone. All alone in a single bed dressed with her sheets and her pillows and surrounded by her childhood things. All of which made it impossible to sleep. Impossible to relax.

It was like being tortured. Being so close to her, surrounded by her, but unable to touch her. It would be better to be sleeping under a tree somewhere far away.

With a groan, he gave up on sleep and got out

of bed, snapping on the light. He moved to a big old chest of drawers and looked at the photos on top—photos of Rosa growing up.

There was one of her with a gap-toothed smile and pigtails at school. Even then her eyes had been beyond beautiful. Another showed her flanked by her brothers, all on bikes. Rosa had been a young teenager then, wearing shorts and a checked shirt, and there was a view of coastal cliffs and sea behind her. A family holiday by the sea. Another one had been taken of her between her mother and father.

Vittorio picked it up. Roberto was right. Rosa looked like a younger version of Maria. He touched a finger to her cheek and growled softly in the night. Soon she would be his. Soon there would be no more room for playing this game of look-but-don't-touch. Soon they would share a bed and much, much more.

And he thought of what Rosa's father had said to him, *'You will never be bored.'*

He believed him.

But, *Dio*, meanwhile he burned.

CHAPTER FIFTEEN

VITTORIO DIDN'T HAVE time to visit Andachstein and deliver the news to his father personally, but he was selfish enough not to want to miss his reaction when he heard the details of his marriage. He had Enrico set his father up to expect a video call the evening they returned to Venice.

At the appointed time Vittorio called, and a few moments later his father appeared on his screen, waving away his secretary. 'Yes, yes, I can manage this now, Enrico.'

Vittorio smiled. 'I've got news, Father.'

Guglielmo grunted as he turned his attention to the screen, and Vittorio could see his patience was already wearing thin.

'There's only one piece of news I'm interested in hearing, so this had better be good.'

'Then you're in luck. I'm getting married.'

'Huh,' he snorted. 'About time. I was hoping I might finally hear something once I had Enrico draw up that list. Who is it, then? Or have you finally managed to sort out your differences with the Contessa.'

'I'm not marrying Sirena.' The words were

more satisfying than he'd expected. Far more satisfying.

'No?' The old Prince rubbed his jaw. 'I'm not sure how Sebastiano is going to take that.'

His father's surprise quickly turned to resignation, as Vittorio had suspected it would. Prince Guglielmo's friend's disappointment was not his most pressing concern. Getting his son married and producing heirs was. Just who provided those heirs was incidental.

'Then who is the lucky woman?'

'Her name is Rosa Ciavarro.'

His father frowned. 'I don't recall seeing anyone on Enrico's list by the name of Ciavarro.'

'She wasn't on Enrico's list. Her family come from the village of Zecce in the south of Italy.'

'A village, you say? Then who is her father?'

'Roberto Ciavarro.'

His father shook his head and looked even more perplexed. Vittorio smiled. He could enjoy letting his father fruitlessly search for connections, but then again there would also be a great deal of satisfaction in revealing the truth.

'I believe he runs the local gas station and motor vehicle repair shop. I hear his speciality is servicing Piaggio Apes.'

Colour flooded his father's cheeks, but to his credit he didn't blow. He was used to being baited by his son.

Vittorio let the news sink in for a second, before he offered, 'Apes are those three-wheel trucks that zip down the narrow laneways carrying produce to market.'

'I know what they are!' his father growled, and his son could almost feel the old man's temperature escalate. 'Don't treat me like an idiot.'

The old man looked upwards to the ceiling, almost as if he was hoping for divine intervention. When that didn't come, he sighed. 'So tell me,' he said, with the air of someone who couldn't be shocked any more than he already had been, 'what does this Rosa do?'

'She works in a hotel in Venice.'

His father swallowed, looking pained. 'Dare I ask in what capacity?'

'She's a maid. A cleaner.'

Closed eyes met that response, along with lips pressed together tightly before they parted enough to say, 'A peasant. You want to marry a peasant. Is this some kind of joke?'

Vittorio knew that he'd well and truly blown that part of his brief. His bride was supposed to be the right kind of woman—someone eligible, from their own social strata, and preferably from the list Enrico had drawn up.

'Because I can tell you it's not funny from where I'm sitting. Can't you for once be serious about your responsibilities?'

Vittorio bristled. 'I've never been more serious about anything, Father. I'm going to marry Rosa.'

His father threw up his hands. 'What on earth for? I suppose you're going to get stars in your eyes and tell me you love the girl.'

'Of course I don't love her. When did this family ever marry for love?'

Guglielmo snorted. It was an agreement of sorts. An acknowledgement of the root cause of all that had been wrong with Vittorio's family. The age-old resentment that lay festering in Vittorio's gut sent up curling tendrils of bitterness. When had love ever come into anything this family did?

'Then why?'

'Because she's pregnant.'

His father shrugged, waving one hand in the air. 'Is that all? It happens. One might say with someone of your ilk it's an occupational hazard. You have the morals of a common alley cat, after all.'

'Perhaps, given my title, not quite so common.'

'Might as well be.' The aging Prince sniffed. 'Anyway, a mere pregnancy still doesn't mean you have to marry the wench. An heir is no good to us if it turns out to be a g—'

'She's having a boy.'

For the first time Vittorio saw his father pause and show just the slightest modicum of interest.

The older man's eyes narrowed as he wheeled back, his gimlet eyes focused hard on his screen as he stroked his beard again. 'You're sure of that?'

'That's what the blood test results said.'

His father sighed and rested his head on his hand. 'But still…a commoner. A peasant, no less.'

'This is the twenty-first century, Father—think about it. The press will lap it up. It's a fairy-tale romance: the Prince and the maid…the ordinary girl who becomes a princess. And a royal baby as the icing on the cake. It's got newspapers and women's magazines across the world written all over it. And when has Andachstein ever had such good press coverage? Think what it will do for our economy. Our hotels and casinos will be filled to overflowing.'

'They're already filled in summer.'

'We'll build more, and those will be full in winter too.'

His father continued to trouble his neat white triangle of a beard, his expression conflicted, before his chin suddenly went up, jerking his beard out of his fingers. 'Do you have a picture of this girl?'

Vittorio pulled out his phone, finding the picture of Rosa he hadn't been able to resist taking that day on the gondola—the one with her dark eyes lit up and her cupid's-bow lips smiling, the wind scattering tendrils of her dark hair across her face. It was a picture that showed Rosa in all her unguarded beauty, raw and innocent—though he knew that she wasn't as innocent as she appeared.

He'd seen to that.

He held it to the screen, saw his father's eyes narrowing as he surveyed the photo, his fingers now more contemplative on his neat beard, and breathed a sigh of relief, knowing that she'd just passed one almighty test. Clearly his father agreed that Rosa would at least pass muster as a princess.

'She'll need instruction,' his father decreed. 'In grooming and, no doubt, in deportment. And she'll need education on the history of the principality and her future role and duties within it.'

Vittorio nodded as he pocketed the phone. 'She'll get it.'

'She's got a lot to catch up on before she can be let loose in public.'

'I said, she'll get it.'

'See that she does. I mean…' his father sighed before continuing '…a simple girl, plucked from a village…'

'Did I *say* she was simple?'

His father paused. 'You're right. She managed to get herself pregnant by a prince, didn't she?'

It was Vittorio's turn to shake his head. 'Father,

for the record, she had no idea I was a prince. And she didn't get herself pregnant. *I* got her pregnant.'

Guglielmo waved his hand in the air dismissively. 'Yes, yes, a technicality. But it happened, and it proves she's a breeder. At least that takes care of who you're going to marry.'

Vittorio couldn't prevent the smile that followed his dinosaur of a father's words. 'Was that congratulations, Father? Because I can almost believe you consented to this marriage.'

The old Prince sniffed as he looked away from the screen and started shuffling his papers.

'I agree to this marriage,' he said, without looking up. 'Given that it is the only option I am apparently going to be presented with. But that does not mean I have to celebrate it.' He looked back at the screen, a look of confusion on his face, and then he yelled over his shoulder. 'Enrico! How do I turn this cursed contraption off?'

CHAPTER SIXTEEN

ROSA WAS ALMOST looking forward to the next few weeks of wedding planning. She'd called Chiara while Vittorio was speaking with his father and given her the news, asking her to be her bridesmaid. She imagined they'd spend evenings together in their apartment, poring over bridal designs. She even entertained tentative plans to sew her own gown. There was enough time, if she could settle on a design and find the right fabric. And if her mother couldn't be there in person, Rosa felt, then at least her sewing machine could provide the magical means of sewing Rosa's wedding gown together.

But it seemed things didn't operate that way when you were going to marry a prince.

Vittorio returned from his call, looking smug and well satisfied, and announced that her time was up. He was moving her into the *palazzo* the very next day, in preparation for the wedding and her move to Andachstein.

Rosa dug her heels in. 'I don't see why.'

'There's every reason why. Because you're now my fiancée, and I can't guarantee your safety while you stay in that basement hovel you call a home.'

'Safety?' she said, really wishing her voice hadn't squeaked.

'You're going to be a princess, Rosa. As soon as the official announcement is made you're going to have people lining up wanting a piece of you. Reporters, the paparazzi, even conmen. All sorts of hangers-on.'

Maybe he was laying it on thick, but he hadn't been in a very good mood lately, and she had a lot to do with that.

'I've tolerated your obstinacy long enough. I can't protect you while you live in the basement of a hotel, where anyone and everyone can just walk in unchallenged. You'll be safer here.'

'I don't call it obstinacy. I call it independence.'

'Call it what you like. It's coming to an end. You're moving into the *palazzo*.'

'What about Chiara?' Rosa said, because there was no way she wanted to be in the sprawling *palazzo* alone with Vittorio but for a sprinkling of staff. It wasn't as if she had super powers. There was no way she was going to be able to stick to her guns and resist him until the wedding without help.

'If it means you'll do what I ask,' he conceded grumpily, 'then Chiara can come too.'

'I didn't think you were *asking*.' She sniffed. 'It sounded more like an order to me.'

He cursed under his breath. *Dio*, a man needed the patience of Job. But then, hadn't her father and brothers warned him?

'Okay,' he said, 'that's the first thing.'

'There's more?'

'I've organised sketches from some of the best designers to be delivered, so you can work out who you'd like to design and create your gown.'

'What if I want to make it myself?'

'Come on, Chiara—this isn't some cheap knock-off you'll be wearing when you walk down the aisle. This is going to be televised all over Europe and possibly the world. Do you want that kind of pressure?'

'I don't make cheap knock-offs.'

He held up his hands. 'Fine. Only I don't think you're going to have much free time in the next few weeks anyway.'

'Why?' she asked, her arms crossed against her chest. 'When you've already made me give up my job?'

'Because Enrico—my father's secretary—is preparing several volumes for you to study on the history, constitution and governance of Andachstein.'

'That sounds like bags of fun.'

'You'll need to be familiar with it all by the

time you're required to attend and speak at official functions.'

'What functions?' She hadn't spoken in public since she'd been at school, and even in front of her school friends she'd been a bundle of nerves.

'Lots of them. The people have missed having a princess. My mother was patron of the children's hospital and at least a dozen other charitable organisations besides. You'll be expected to fill that role.'

She kicked up her chin. 'So I agree to marry you and I lose my life.'

'It's not all bad, Rosa,' he said, gritting his teeth. 'You gain me.'

'Huh,' she said, and turned away.

It wasn't an easy thing to do. She'd fallen a little bit in love with him that magical night of Carnevale and nothing had changed that. Not the fact that he'd disappeared for six weeks, because he'd been honest about that. And not the fact that he'd quietly neglected to inform her that he was a prince until it was too late and she'd already discovered she was pregnant.

Because she hadn't fallen a little bit in love with a prince. She'd fallen for the man. Vittorio. And lately he reminded her more and more of how he'd been that night. There was an edge to him, magnetic and powerful, bordering on dangerous, and the knowledge that she'd put it there by defying him was exciting. Intoxicating.

She didn't need an aphrodisiac. She still dreamed of him at night, still replayed their love scenes, every touch and every sound. She still longed to make love to him again and again.

But she wanted all of him this time. She didn't just want his lust. She wanted his affection. More than that, she yearned for his love.

Come the wedding, she would be bound to him. They would be man and wife under the sight of God and she would take her place in the marital bed. And she would enjoy it.

But for now the only thing she had control of, the only ace she had up her sleeve, was her resolve to keep Vittorio at arm's length. So he might look beyond the sex and see the woman she was.

If Vittorio had thought having Rosa residing in the *palazzo* might weaken her resolve and make her more accessible and more amenable to his affections, and if he'd thought he might pay her a little nocturnal visit, he had another think coming.

Rosa and Chiara were moving in amidst a whirl of excitement—mostly on Chiara's part. She was running up and down the stairs, shrieking at just about everything. But that wasn't the worst of it. He'd thought the move was taking longer than he'd expected, and he'd gone to see what was happening, and found his staff carrying beds around.

'What the hell is going on?' he bellowed as he watched them grappling with an ancient four-poster bed.

'Calm down,' snapped Rosa. 'There's no need to shout.'

'Just answer my question.'

She shrugged on a grin. 'We're simply moving this bed into my room.'

'You've already got a bed in your room.'

'But there isn't a bed for Chiara.'

'She has an entire bedroom at her disposal.'

'Oh, but Vittorio,' she said, 'we *like* sharing a room. How else are we going to talk late into the night?'

'You could always phone each other,' he said.

She laughed. 'That would be silly when we're in the same building.' She smiled up at him. 'Don't worry,' she said. 'It's only until the wedding.'

And she leaned up to press the lightest of kisses to his lips. A touch. A tease. A peck. And nowhere near enough. He tried to catch her and pull her close, but she'd whirled away, quicksilver in motion, before he could get hold of her.

He grumped back to his suite.

Only until the wedding.

He wanted her. He burned with wanting her.

But what irked him more was that he could not help but admire her.

'Not a doormat,' Marcello had said.

Not a chance.

She was like a wily negotiator, the way she made her quiet demands. And there was no budging her. She would not be swayed. But she was definitely tempted. Otherwise why would she move Chiara into her room? She didn't trust herself and Chiara was her wall.

It was infuriating. She was defending the terms of their agreement like a tigress defending its cub.

He smiled a little at that. Whatever kind of father he turned out to be, he knew Rosa would make a good mother. He'd seen her holding her tiny niece and nephews. He'd seen the way she doted on them. And maybe, just maybe, she would help him be the kind of father he wished he'd had.

He sighed as he went to his room and rummaged through his closet for gym clothes. He could last. It seemed he had no choice but to burn off some energy in more conventional ways. But, hell, a man could burst with wanting her.

CHAPTER SEVENTEEN

Rosa rubbed the bridge of her nose and sighed as she studied the dusty tome in the library.

'What's wrong?' asked Chiara, who was lying on a chaise longue nearby and reading a bridal magazine.

'The constitution of Andachstein. It's the most boring thing I've ever read in my life. I'm never going to get through all these volumes. No wonder Vittorio said I wouldn't have enough time to make my own gown.'

'Hey,' Chiara said, flicking through the pages, 'Vittorio wants you to have a designer gown, and I say go for it. There's only a few weeks until the wedding. You'd be crazy to try and rush it yourself when a designer would have an entire team of seamstresses at their disposal. You can always make something else for the wedding. A garter for your leg, or Vittorio's bow tie.' She looked up suddenly. 'Do princes even wear bow ties to their own weddings?'

'Who knows?' said Rosa, turning back to her tome. 'Don't they usually wear medals or a sash?'

Chiara shrugged next to her, and for a while there was silence but for the flicking of pages—

Chiara's magazine pages, because it was taking for ever for Rosa to make her way through even one of the pages in her turgid tome. She sighed again.

Chiara looked up. 'Tell you what. How about we take a look at some of those sketches from the designers Vittorio organised? You've barely looked at them and you don't have long to make a decision.'

'Yeah…' Rosa said, rubbing her forehead with her hand. She had barely looked at them because she'd had her heart set on designing and making her own gown, but time was slipping by and there was so much to do. So much to read. 'Maybe you're right.'

'Great,' said Chiara, jumping up. 'You could do with a break. I'll go get them. Be right back.'

Rosa sat back in her chair and closed her eyes. Her head ached with the effort of trying to make sense of the medieval mumbo jumbo she was reading. How was she ever supposed to get a handle on it all?

'Rosa?'

She opened her eyes with a start to see Vittorio standing in the wide doorway.

'Are you all right?'

Her heart skipped in her chest as he strode towards her purposefully, like a powerful cat, all grace and barely leashed power. In a soft winter-white sweater that hugged his sculpted chest and fitted black trousers he looked amazing, and her hands ached to reach out and trace the skinscape of his body through the luxurious wool.

'I'm fine,' she said.

But her skin was tingling, and she was feeling strangely vulnerable. It was the first time they'd been alone together since she'd moved into the *palazzo*. The first time she hadn't had Chiara's presence to shield her and give her the confidence to pretend to be unmoved and light-hearted.

There was no pretending to be unmoved now. Her mouth had gone dry.

'Then what is the problem?'

You, she wanted to say. She looked around him. *Where was Chiara?*

'These damned books,' she said. 'They're so boring. I can't be expected to read them all.'

'You don't like the history of Andachstein?'

'I don't see a lot to interest me so far, no.'

He smiled and looked around too, and she knew he was checking for Chiara. His smile widened when he didn't find her.

'Then maybe you are starting in the wrong place. Andachstein has a rich and fascinating history.' He rounded the desk. 'Perhaps I can show you.'

'It's okay,' she said, even as he leaned over her and examined the volumes on the desk. She felt his heat wrap around her, caress her like a breeze stirring a crop of grain, sparking her sensitive nerve-endings, coaxing her nipples into hard peaks.

'Have you read about the lace industry? That would interest you, surely?'

'Andachstein has a lace industry?'

He nodded and plucked one volume from the collection on the desk and opened it to a particular page. 'Here,' he said, pointing to where there were some photographs of various patterns of lace, some delicately shell-like, others resembling flowers. 'The then Princess Rienna wanted to open schools to girls. She invited a group of nuns to move from Bruges to Andachstein and start a school. They brought with them their lace-making skills and passed them on to the girls and women of the principality.'

Rosa tried to ignore his presence at her shoulder and concentrate on his words, but she could feel the puff of his breath in her hair and against her skin and it was all she could do not to turn her face to his.

'She sounds,' she said, trying to stop her voice sounding tremulous, 'very forward-thinking.'

'She was. She wanted to do something to repay Andachstein for saving her life and she saw this as a way.'

This time her head did turn to his—just a little.

Her gaze caught the strength of his jaw, the curve of his lips and strong nose, and she looked away again, feeling dizzy. Breathless. She hadn't been this close to Vittorio for so long, and the masculine scent of him was like a drug.

Her eyes were fixed on the pages in front of her, her hands flat on the desk lest they move of their own volition towards him. *Where the hell was Chiara?*

'How was she saved by Andachstein?'

'Rienna was a Celtic princess, taken prisoner on a pirate ship bound for Constantinople. Various accounts say she had eyes the colour of sapphires. She'd been kidnapped from her home and intended as a gift for the Sultan, destined to join his harem as one of his concubines. There was a storm and the pirate ship got blown off course into Andachstein waters, where a naval vessel attacked the ship and freed the Princess. The girl's father was so grateful he offered her to the then Prince, whose own wife had died in childbirth, along with their stillborn son, one year earlier. Princess Rienna went on to bear him eight children, and her intensely blue eyes have been passed down through the generations ever since.'

This time Rosa did turn her head—all the way. She looked up at his cobalt eyes, entranced by the story of pirates and Celtic princesses and times long gone. 'Will our son have those same eyes?'

He turned those eyes down at her, and she felt her insides quiver.

'If he is my son.'

'You know he is your son.'

'I do,' he said, and his eyes were so intense that her breath hitched and she wasn't sure for a moment whether he was answering the same question. She knew that if he asked her in this moment if she wanted to make love to him she would utter those same two words.

His lips were closer. How had that happened when she hadn't taken her eyes from him? His lips were only a breath from hers now, the time that separated them no more than a heartbeat.

She was going to kiss him. There was nothing surer, no matter the bargain they'd made or the terms he'd agreed to. *Her* terms—except they didn't seem to matter now.

All that mattered was that Vittorio was here now.

'I found them!' Chiara breezed into the room and stopped dead.

Beside her Rosa was almost certain she heard Vittorio growl.

'Sorry, am I interrupting something?'

Rosa sprang up from her chair. 'No. Vittorio was just filling me in on some of Andachstein's history. Weren't you, Vittorio?'

'Something like that,' he said, pushing himself upright.

'Chiara and I are going to look at those sketches and choose a designer,' Rosa said, talking too fast but unable to stop herself. 'You were right, of course, I will never have time to make something myself.'

'In that case,' said Vittorio, looking from one woman to the other, 'I will leave you to it.'

And he departed.

'What was that about?' asked Chiara.

'Nothing,' said Rosa, both grateful and annoyed at Chiara's sudden reappearance. 'Show me the designs.'

Chiara looked as if she didn't believe her, but then her excitement returned. 'I think I've found the perfect gown. There are others too, but what do you think?'

Rosa took the sketch. It was an off-the-shoulder gown with a fitted bodice, three-quarter sleeves and a back finished with a row of tiny pearl buttons that dropped much lower. There was a long train and a cathedral veil trimmed in lace. Swatches of the suggested fabric—a white Shantung silk—and a sample of the veil were attached.

There were no embellishments apart from the row of tiny buttons at the back. Nothing fancy. Nothing fussy. Just sleek, unfettered design.

Rosa felt a zing of excitement. 'It's beautiful.'

Chiara grinned. 'It would look magic on you. You'll only be three months pregnant by then, and you shouldn't be showing, but even if you are it will be hidden by the cut of the skirt.'

Rosa quickly flipped through the pages to see the other designs. She stopped at one—a gown made entirely of lace. Andachstein lace. Her thumb fingered the swatches while she was thinking.

'You'd rather have a gown made in lace?' Chiara said.

Rosa smiled. 'No, but it's given me an idea.'

CHAPTER EIGHTEEN

ANDACHSTEIN'S CATHEDRAL WAS a grand affair on the headland overlooking the harbour, with origins that harked back to Roman times. The cathedral had been built and ruined and rebuilt over the ages, until the existing building had been erected from the ruins some time in the fourteenth century and extended half a dozen times since.

A testament to the architect's love and knowledge of arches, the cathedral boasted a long central aisle and a Gothic rose window at one end, with a golden domed nave at the other. Stained-glass windows had been added over the centuries.

Rosa knew all this as she stood at the entrance, her father by her side and Chiara behind her, to straighten her train and stop her veil blowing away. Vittorio had brought her here for a rehearsal, and she'd been stunned then by the magnificence and history of the place. The tiny chapel in the village where she'd grown up, where they'd said goodbye to her mother, seemed like a dot in a dusty landscape in comparison.

And now, with the music from the pipe organ sweeping out of the interior, rising to the moment where she would have to enter the cathedral, Rosa had a moment of self-doubt.

What was she doing here?

She'd been thrust into this position because of one passionate night that had been meant to be the end. She was marrying a man whose child she carried. They were about to exchange vows declaring that they would love and cherish each other, that they would forsake all others.

But did Vittorio love her? Would he ever love her enough to forsake all others? She wanted so much what her mother and father had shared. She wanted it all. Marriage, family, and love at the heart of it.

What if it never happened?

What if Vittorio never loved her?

She wouldn't be able to bear it.

She'd wither slowly from the inside out.

Her father must have noticed her shallow breathing. He patted the hand tucked under his arm.

'All right?' he asked, his forehead creased into a frown, concern lining his eyes.

She took a deep breath and found a weak smile to reassure him. Of course she was. She had to be. She thought of her unborn child, of the things she would be denying him if she turned her back on all this now, and she couldn't do it. Not just to satisfy her own personal needs and longings.

She smiled up at her father again. 'Bridal jitters,' she said. 'I'm fine.'

He kissed her then, and told her, 'You look beautiful today. No father could be prouder.'

Rosa gave a tremulous smile. How could she not look beautiful today? Her gown was divine. She'd decided on a simple sleek design, similar to the one in the sketch Chiara had shown her, and together with the designer had decided on a champagne-coloured silk. A long veil edged with Andachstein lace was held in place with a tiara that had belonged to Vittorio's mother and boasted a magnificent Brazilian topaz.

The whole ensemble was so utterly perfect she was glad she'd been talked out of trying to make a dress herself. Besides, it had given her time to tackle some other projects.

'My only regret is that your mother isn't here to witness this moment.' Her father gave a sad, soft smile, his eyes glazed. 'She would be so proud, and I know she is smiling down on you like the sun is today.'

'Don't make me cry,' Rosa pleaded, dabbing at her eyes.

And then there was no time for tears as the music shifted up a notch.

'There's our cue,' her father said as a footman gave him a signal. 'Are you ready?'

Rosa sucked in a breath, smiled weakly and nodded. 'Ready,' she said.

The sun through the stained-glass windows drenched the waiting congregation in puddles of coloured light. Dust motes glowed like sparks of gold in the vast space above. Either side of her were wall-to-wall smiles. But she didn't have eyes for any of it.

For there at the front, waiting for her, stood Vittorio, tall and proud. Her breath caught in her throat. Because, outfitted in the black dress uniform of the Andachstein Guard, trimmed with gold braid and buttons, once again he looked just as he had that first night—more like a warrior, or a warlord, or even a god, than any mere mortal.

He watched her approach…didn't take his eyes off her as she took every slow step down the aisle. He was smiling a little, she noticed as they grew closer, just enough to soften the hard angles and planes of his warrior face, and in his eyes she saw approval and satisfaction, desire and maybe even a little wonderment.

But was there room in them for a little love? She wanted with all her heart to see love there.

At the last moment she noticed her family, all smiles as they passed, and there was Prince Guglielmo watching too, wearing his perpetual frown and as beady-eyed as ever.

She drew level with her groom and he offered

her his arm, his amazing blue eyes searching her face.

Beautiful, he mouthed, and her heart gave a little kick that had her trembling.

Tonight she would lie with this man in the marital bed. Tonight they would consummate this unlikely marriage and be as one. All this time Vittorio had thought *he* was the one missing out, the one hard done by, but he had no idea of the sacrifice she'd made in not giving in to her desires. She wanted to be back in his arms more than he knew. She'd longed for this night, this intimacy, this connection. But she was afraid of it too, and of what it might mean.

She'd told Vittorio that she was worried that this marriage would mean losing her independence. But tonight she knew she was in danger of losing herself.

The ceremony began. The priest spoke his solemn words, music soared at intervals, and a choir filled with what sounded like angels turned hymns into the sweetest sounds she had ever heard.

Rosa felt as if she was standing outside herself, watching on. How could it be her, Rosa Ciavarro, from a tiny village in the south of Italy, standing there marrying a prince? It was unbelievable. Surreal.

When they exchanged their vows it was Vittorio who sounded confident and assured in the soaring space, whose voice didn't waver. It was Vittorio who looked her in the eye and made her want to believe that some part of this was not just an act of convenience, going through the motions, that some part of it was real.

And then they were pronounced husband and wife, and their lips met in a kiss that had her doubting again. Because it was more business-like than affectionate. Sealing the deal.

He walked her down the aisle a married woman—a princess—and she felt numb. Shell-shocked.

In a touch of unexpected informality the guests spilled out of the cathedral behind them, full of congratulations and good wishes for the newly-weds. She found herself separated from Vittorio as they were tugged in different directions, but even that didn't matter because everyone was so happy.

Until a woman latched on to her arm. 'I sup-pose I should congratulate you,' she said.

Rosa turned. There was no mistaking the vampish woman, even though Cleopatra had turned honey-blonde since she'd last seen her. 'Thank you, Contessa.'

'I'll let you into a little secret, though,' the woman whispered as she air-kissed Rosa's cheeks. 'He'll never love you. His lot are incapable of it.'

She smiled as she stepped back. 'So you might as well lose those stars in your eyes right now.'

Rosa gasped, too stunned to speak. Was she that obvious? Was she so transparent that everyone could see the longing to be loved written plain on her face?

And then her brothers and their wives and children were swarming around her and she was surrounded by joy and love in abundance, and she almost felt greedy that she wanted more when she already had more than some people had in a lifetime.

'Where's my wife?' she heard a booming voice say over the crowd.

My wife.

A zing of electricity sent shockwaves down her spine. Possession. It was there in his words, there in his tone.

Nothing to do with love. It was all about lust, and anticipation for the evening ahead. She knew because the time had come and she felt it too.

And then the crowd parted and Vittorio was there, larger than life. His jewel-coloured eyes lit up when he saw her. 'Ah, there you are, my Princess. We have a state reception to get to,' he said. 'But first—'

He swept her up in his arms and kissed her, to the cheers of the crowd. Not like the kiss he'd given her in the cathedral—that one had been warm but brief. Sweet. Official, even. This was a kiss that spoke of barely restrained passion, of desire that was about to be taken off the leash. A kiss that left her breathless and weak-kneed and pulsing in places that knew how Vittorio could make them feel and wanted it as much as she did.

Maybe tonight she should just let herself be possessed. Maybe tonight should be all about desire. About slaking mutual need and lust.

And tomorrow, and all the tomorrows to come, maybe then she could worry about love.

The party was still raging, the orchestra still playing and wedding guests still dancing, when Vittorio approached Rosa and growled softly in her ear, 'It's time.'

Rosa had been enjoying herself, having found ten minutes to be with her family. She'd smiled when Chiara had taken to the dance floor yet again with Marcello. Marvelled when Prince Guglielmo had accompanied Sirena to the floor for a waltz. But mostly she'd just enjoyed being in the company of her family again. Soon they'd have to return to Zecce and she'd miss them.

But now Vittorio was telling her it was time. She trembled. His breath was warm against her skin, his own scent flavoured with the cognac he'd had with coffee. It was a powerful combination. Addictive.

Her heart was thumping in her chest as they made their exit and he walked her down the long passageway, their footsteps ringing out on the stone floor, the sounds of the reception given up to silence.

She didn't talk.

There were no words. And even if there had been, her throat was too tight.

He didn't talk.

He didn't rush. His steps were measured. Un-hurried.

It was nerve-racking.

Excruciating.

A flight of stairs took them to the next level and then into his apartments. By the time he opened the door to his softly lit suite her nerves were stretched to breaking point. She knew her things had been moved into his suite while the formali-ties took place today, but this was the first time she'd seen his room. As she took it in, the dark wood furniture, the big leather sofas and the wide expanse of the massive four-poster bed, one word immediately sprang to mind.

Masculine.

He closed the solid door behind them with an equally solid *thunk*. She jumped at the sound.

'Nervous, my Princess?' he said, close behind her.

She'd dispensed with her veil before the reception, and now there was nothing between the puff of his breath and the nape of her neck. So close that she could feel his heat.

'It's been a long day,' she said.

She would have taken a step away, but his hands were already at her shoulders, and his lips—she gasped—his lips were pressed to that place where his breath had touched. Warmth suffused her flesh and threatened to turn her bones to jelly.

'Did I tell you,' he whispered, his thumbs stroking the bare skin of her back, 'how beautiful you look today?'

She nodded. He had—though not in so many words. And he'd made her believe it.

She'd expected he'd turn her then, and pull her into his kiss, but instead his thumbs traced a line down the V at her back, his touch sparking fires under her skin.

'And I love this dress,' he said, his fingers reaching the point where the row of tiny buttons began. 'But now it's time to do something I've been itching to do all evening.'

She felt his fingers settle on the top button. His long fingers on his big hands. She wanted to protest—he would never manage to undo the tiny buttons, she would have to call for a maid to help.

But she felt the first button give. His lips pressed to the other side of her neck and she felt the brush of his hair against her skin and breathed him in. She would have turned herself then, to kiss him, to replay that wondrous deep kiss he'd given her after they were married, but he wouldn't let her, and his surprisingly nimble fingers were still working away at the buttons.

But, as with his measured steps, he didn't rush. He took his own sweet time, pressing his lips to the skin of her exposed back as his fingers moved still lower, until he reached the small of her back, where the touch of his fingers tripped a secret cord that pulled tight inside her so that her muscles clenched. His hands were nowhere near her breasts, but she felt them swell, her nipples turning to bullets.

The gown was loosening around her. 'You don't have to do them all,' she said, surprised to hear how husky her voice sounded.

He chuckled softly against her skin and the sensation reverberated through her flesh and down to her bones.

'You sound impatient, my Princess.'

If she wasn't mistaken, his voice had gone down an octave.

'Surely you don't want me to hurry the most special night of your life?'

She was, and she did,—but she wasn't about to admit that.

She was at fever pitch when she felt the last

button give. She felt his hands slide down inside her dress to cup her cheeks, and then sweep up her sides to cup her breasts. Breath caught in her throat. *At last!*

Then, and only then, he turned her and lifted her face to meet his. Lips met lips. Mouth slanted across mouth. Breath intermingled. And it was like returning to a fantasy place where her every dream came true.

She groaned, protesting into their kiss as he angled her away, but only to ease her arms from the sleeves and let the gown fall in a pool at her feet.

'*Dio...*' he said, looking down at her, taking in the tiny scraps of delicate lace that barely covered her breasts and the tiny triangle that concealed the V at the apex of her thighs. Thigh-high lace-topped stockings completed her underwear. 'What are you doing to me? All day long and you were as good as naked under that gown.'

Rosa felt empowered. 'Do you like them? I made them myself.' She could see by the flare and the heat in his eyes what his answer would be before she asked the question.

'Like them?' he said, his fingers tracing the intricate gold patterns in the lace.

'It's lace made by the Andachstein Lace-Makers' Guild. I ordered it especially.'

He lifted his eyes to hers. 'Did they have any idea what you planned to do with their lace?'

He sounded as if he had a lump in his throat that it was difficult to talk past. She smiled. 'Do you think they'd mind?'

'I'm not sure, but I've got a pretty good idea you've just committed an offence against the moral fabric of Andachstein society.'

'You'd charge me?'

'No, but only on one condition.'

'Which is?'

'You let me take them off.'

She smiled, hope creeping into her heart. 'I thought you'd never ask.'

He gave a roar of triumph and swept her into his arms, placing her reverently on the bed before shedding his dress uniform. Shoes and other garments were going everywhere, until he stood naked before her, proud and erect. She gasped. Her memories had failed her. Her dreams hadn't done him justice. The man was magnificent.

And now he leaned over her, kissing her lips, his big hands in her hair, cupping her cheek, following the curve of her shoulders and seeking the clasp for her bra, finding it.

He slid the fabric away and drew back. Air hissed through his teeth before he dipped his head again and drew one nipple into his hot mouth. So hot. Her back arched as he suckled, sending spears of pleasure straight to her core, and then again when he turned his attentions to her other breast.

'So beautiful,' he said, before he scooped his hands lower, over the curve of her abdomen and the flare of her hips.

She was panting when he dipped his head and pressed his lips over the place where their unborn child lay. So gentle. So tender. She wanted more. Needed more.

But he bypassed the heated place that screamed out for his attention, and moved straight to her ankles, sliding off first one high-heeled shoe and then the other, before kissing his way up her calf and then her inner thigh, until she was molten and pulsing with need.

'Vittorio!' she cried.

'I know,' he said, his hands curled into the sides of the scrap of lace that was all that separated them. 'I feel it too,' he said, and slowly drew them down her legs.

She was burning up before he slipped a hand between her thighs and coaxed them apart. She was on fire before he slipped one finger between her lips and brushed past that tight nub of nerve-endings, inciting it to fever-pitch.

'So hot,' he said on a groan.

'Vittorio!'

'I know,' he said again, soothing her as he knelt between her legs, his big hands palming her body, her breasts, her arms, her belly, her legs, as if he couldn't get enough of the feel of her. He poised himself over her, kissed her deep and hard, devouring her like a starving man who had been served up a feast.

She welcomed him at her entrance. Cried out with the contact, with the agony and the ecstasy of it, with the frustration and the promise. Cried out again when he surged into her, filling her, pausing before he withdrew and surged in again. This was skin against skin, his skin against hers in the most intimate of contacts, and it was pure magic.

She was already on the brink, already close, when he dipped his mouth and tugged on one peaked nipple. A shooting star flashed behind her eyes, one star that became two, and then another, until her world hurtled through the path of a meteor shower and everything was light and fire and the brilliance of feeling.

She was still spinning back down to earth, still finding her place back in the world and feeling warm and delicious when she said it.

It wasn't her fault—not entirely—but she was lulled by Vittorio's big body next to hers, his strong arms still around her, their legs interwoven, and they seemed the most natural words in the world to well up inside her at that moment.

She pressed her lips to his magnificent chest,

felt the squeeze of his arm at her shoulders. *'I love you.'*

She felt him stiffen. Felt every muscle in his body tense. Felt him pull away.

'Vittorio…?'

'No,' he said, his body stiff as he rolled away. 'Don't say that. I didn't ask you to say that.'

Only then did she realise that she'd spoken out loud the words branding her heart.

'Why? What's wrong? I know it's too soon. But it's how I feel.' She reached out a hand to his shoulder, feeling as if she was losing him. 'I can't help how I feel.'

He sprang from the bed. 'Did I ask you to love me? Don't love me,' he said. 'Never love me. Because I can't love you back.'

'Vittorio—'

'Don't you remember? I was a bastard to you at Carnevale. I used you.'

'What? That's all in the past. We're beyond that. Why are you dragging it out now?'

'Because you need to remember the kind of person I am. I don't love people, Rosa.'

'But now… Surely now that we're married—'

'You *know* why I married you. If you hadn't been pregnant we wouldn't be married now. It's got nothing to do with love.'

His words stung. So what if he was speaking the truth? It was his attitude that slashed at her soul. 'But it could. What is to stop me loving you and you loving me? It's normal. It's natural.'

'Not in my world!' he yelled. 'Do you think I can simply flick a switch? So don't love me. Don't ever tell me you love me. And don't expect anything of me. It's not going to happen.'

'You just made love to me—'

'It was *sex*, Rosa. Just sex! That's all it was. It's time you understood that. That's all it can ever be.'

He stormed out of the room through a side door that slammed heavily in his wake. She heard water running. A shower. And she sensed he wouldn't be back to share her bed tonight.

She sat shell-shocked in the bed, perilously close to tears, her wedding night reduced to ashes, her hopes and dreams in tatters. But she refused to let loose the tears. She took great gulps of air until the urge to cry was suppressed, even as Sirena's words came back to haunt her.

'He'll never love you. His lot aren't capable of it.'

What was Vittorio so afraid of? He'd acted as if it was a curse. A horrid affliction for which there was no cure and death the only release. But there was nothing to fear from love.

And he was wrong, she knew it. He *could* love. A man who had grown up from a boy who would rescue a drowning kitten. A man who rescued strays and the vulnerable. This was not a man devoid of love.

He just didn't know how to show it.

Or maybe he just didn't know how to show it to *her*. Maybe he'd loved his first wife so much that he'd never got over her death.

Rosa was too afraid to ask. That wasn't a conversation she wanted to have on their wedding night.

The new bride sniffed, a new resolution forming in her mind. She knew how to sew. She was good at stitching pieces of fabric together and making something good, something worthwhile. So she would take the tattered shreds of her hopes and dreams and stitch them back together.

Because, despite what Vittorio had told her to do, there was no way she was giving up on her hopes and dreams just yet.

CHAPTER NINETEEN

THE NEW PRINCESS of Andachstein threw herself into her role. She visited the local primary schools and read the children storybooks and every child was entranced. She gave speeches at colleges into which she incorporated her newfound knowledge of the history and the proud heritage of Andachstein.

Wherever she appeared with Vittorio they were mobbed by cheering crowds waving the Andachstein flag. And when the first pictures of her baby bump were snapped and flashed to the world by the media, satisfaction levels regarding the principality went through the roof.

And if Vittorio himself wasn't entirely happy with how things were proceeding, Prince Guglielmo was beside himself. 'You got yourself a gem there, Vittorio,' he said during their weekly meeting. 'An absolute gem.'

Vittorio couldn't disagree. Rosa was proving perfect in the role. She was proving perfect in his bed. This night of their wedding had been an aberration. She'd made no unwanted transgressions since. But then, how could she when she said nothing at all? Sure, she was passionate enough, but they made love without a word from her. It was as if she was there in body, but not in soul.

But wasn't that what he wanted?

'What is the Princess up to today?' his father asked, dragging him out of his misery.

For the first time Vittorio noticed that his father looked a little better. A little younger than he had before. It couldn't all be down to the recent haircut he'd clearly had.

Vittorio leaned one hip against the desk and tossed the crystal paperweight from one hand to the other. It spoke volumes for his father's lighter mood that he barely blinked at Vittorio's audacity. He sighed.

'She's at a meeting of the Lace-Makers Guild. She's asked to become their patron. Apparently the women were delighted to have a patron who is herself a seamstress.'

The old man nodded his approval. 'Her first solo appointment? Impressive. We're not working her too hard, are we?'

'I don't think so.'

But maybe that was the problem, Vittorio mused, looking out of the window at the harbour below. Maybe she was just tired.

He shook his head and turned back to his father. 'Rosa seems to be loving it. And the baby is growing well. Rosa just had her twenty-week scan. All is looking good.'

'Good! So we're still expecting a boy?'

Vittorio smiled. 'That is now beyond doubt.' He'd seen the unmistakable evidence on the screen himself.

The old Prince grunted. 'Excellent.' And then he sighed and walked to stand in front of one of the big picture windows, his hands clasped behind his back. 'Late November, then…' he said, his voice reflective.

'That's what they say.'

'My doctors say there is a new technique. Still risky, but less so.'

For a moment Vittorio searched for this thread in the conversation, and then his father spun around and said, 'I'm thinking I would like to see my grandson growing up. I'm thinking I should tell the doctors to go ahead with my surgery.'

'But still risky?' Vittorio queried.

'Eighty per cent chance of success, they tell me. That sounds better than one hundred per cent chance of death if I don't have it, wouldn't you say?'

Vittorio left his father in unusually high spirits. The chance offered by surgery, he guessed. That would do it.

But then he saw Sirena walking towards him. 'Contessa,' he said.

She smiled. She was dressed in what he'd heard

was called a 'tea dress', all big floral skirts and a tribute to the fifties, right down to the gloves, hat and strappy shoes.

'*Buongiorno*, Vittorio,' she said, stopping to kiss him on both cheeks. 'I hope married life agrees with you.'

'What are you doing here, Contessa?' he asked, sidestepping the question. He'd hoped that now he was married she would set her sights on some other target.

'I have an appointment with Guglielmo.'

'With my father?'

'Well, not really an appointment, as such. We're having a picnic down by the lake. It's such a beautiful day for a picnic, don't you think?' She raised her eyebrows and gave a flutter of her gloved hand. 'I'd better go. He's waiting for me.'

And with a click-clack of her heels she was gone, and Vittorio was left thinking, maybe she already had.

Rosa had enjoyed her first solo appointment. She'd been right to tell Vittorio she could handle this one herself.

The women of the Lace-Makers' Guild had made her so welcome. They'd given her an amazing display of their craft—flashing hands shifting threaded bobbins and pins—and she'd been dazzled by their skills. They'd even given her a lesson in lace-making, and watched patiently while she'd attempted to follow the pattern before declaring that she was much better at using their lace in her sewing projects than creating it. Then they'd all laughed and shared late-morning tea together.

Then they'd presented her with two gifts. One a lace shawl for their baby. So fine and beautiful, with a pattern of doves cleverly tatted through it. And the second a pair of pillowcases for the royal bed. Exquisitely made, they must have taken weeks and weeks to create.

She'd promised them that they would be cherished, even if she couldn't think about her marriage bed without a tinge of sadness. It had been weeks since their marriage—weeks during which she'd said not a word during their lovemaking. Weeks during which she wasn't even sure Vittorio had noticed.

A group of children were waiting with their teachers outside the Lace-Makers' Guild, preschoolers from the nearby kindergarten, huddled under a shady tree, out of the hot July sun. All she wanted to do was be out of the hot sun too, and inside the air-conditioned comfort of her waiting car, being whisked back to the cool confines of the *castello* high above the town, where the summer heat didn't seem to penetrate.

But the children were waiting for her, and she

wasn't about to disappoint them. She knelt down to their level just as a delivery van trundled slowly past, pulling to a stop a few houses up the street. Rosa took no notice of the man who jumped out with a parcel under his arm—she was already talking to the children.

A little boy presented her with a posy of flowers.

A little girl in a wheelchair was wheeled forward to ask a question.

'Can I be a princess when I grow up?' she asked shyly.

Rosa took her small hand in hers, and said, 'You can be anything you want.'

The little girl threw her arms around Rosa's neck and hugged her tight. And Rosa thought that it wasn't so bad, being a princess, even if your husband didn't think he could love you.

Someone shouted something up the road. There was a murmur of concerned voices, and then more shouting, but she was still disentangling herself from the girl's arms when she heard her driver call, 'Your Highness! Watch out!'

Children started shrieking. 'Run this way!' she heard one teacher call.

She turned her head to see her driver lunging for her. But there was something that would beat him. The delivery truck, bearing down on them, with a man futilely chasing after it.

Fight or flight? There was no question.

She pushed the wheelchair as hard as she could and flung herself after it.

CHAPTER TWENTY

VITTORIO WAS FURIOUS by the time he got to the hospital. Furious with himself. He should never have agreed to let Rosa go by herself today. And he was furious with everyone who might have had a part in this.

But most of all he was furious because of all the things he could have said to her and never had. All the things he *should* have said to her. And all the cruel things he'd said to her because he had been so desperate to protect himself.

'What happened?' he demanded of her driver as he marched along the disinfectant-smelling corridor in the hospital. 'I want to know everything that happened and in detail. And then I want to know *how* it happened.'

It was all the chauffeur could do to keep up with him, let alone give him a detailed account of all that had transpired.

'The delivery vehicle is being checked over now,' the man said. 'But it looks like brake failure.'

'On a damned hill, of all places,' Vittorio said, seething, 'and right above where Rosa was standing.'

'The Princess was kneeling down,' said the driver, 'talking to a child in a wheelchair. The child was hugging her. The Princess didn't know what was happening until too late.'

A doctor strode towards them. 'Prince Vittorio, I'm Dr Belosci. I'm looking after the Princess. I'll take you to her. We're prepping her for Theatre now.'

Fear slid down Vittorio's spine.

He dismissed the driver, waiting for him to be out of earshot. 'Is it the baby?' Nobody had told him there was a problem with the baby—but then nobody had mentioned Theatre either.

'No. Didn't they tell you? The baby's fine. It's Her Highness's ankle. A tree took the brunt of the crash, but a tyre snapped free with the force of the collision and caught her on the ankle.'

Breath whooshed out of Vittorio's lungs. 'She's going to be all right, then?'

'They're both going to be fine. Just as soon as we can get that ankle set. Come and see her, and then I'll show you the X-rays.'

The baby was all right, his heartbeat sound and strong. Someone had come and told her that the little girl in the wheelchair had got a bump on the head but was fine. It couldn't be better.

Rosa hugged her baby bump while she drifted in and out of dreamland. She'd told them she didn't want a fuss, that she would be just as happy back in her own bed in the *castello*, but they'd insisted, telling her she was to be attached to a drip and that she needed an operation on her ankle.

And then she'd remembered the pain as she'd waited for the ambulance and thought maybe it was better to be here in hospital after all. At least it was quiet here.

She heard voices coming down the corridor. Loud voices. No—one loud voice and one quieter. No guessing which one was Vittorio's.

She put one hand to her head. *Dio*, why had they had to tell him? Couldn't they have waited until after the operation? The baby was fine. It wasn't as if he wanted to see *her*.

The door to her room creaked open. 'Rosa?' he said.

She turned her head away. 'The baby's fine, Vittorio. Didn't they tell you?'

'Yes, they told me.'

'So, thanks for coming, but don't feel you need to stay. I'm in good hands here.'

'Rosa, I came to see *you*.'

She laughed. Maybe it was the drugs in her drip, or maybe she was just fed up with being silent, but she wasn't going to stay silent any more. 'Nice one, Vittorio, but I don't think so.'

'Rosa——'

She snapped her head around. 'What are you still doing here? Staying long enough to convince the staff we're madly in love, like you pretended to be at our wedding? Well, I don't read the tabloids—and even if I did that fantasy died a death on our wedding night, thanks to you. So I don't need you to stay, Vittorio. I don't *want* you to stay.'

But he didn't leave. Infuriatingly, he sat down in the visitor's chair beside the bed.

'For once and for all, the baby is fine. I'm sure someone here will let you know the moment that changes. Can you please go?'

She heard him sigh, and was about to snap at him again when he said, 'I didn't come here because of the baby.'

'Liar,' she said, but she was curious enough to hear what else he had to say.

'All right. I was worried about the baby. But I came because you'd been hurt and I was worried about you. Because today I realised something that has been staring me in the face for almost as long as we've been together.'

Her heart slammed into her chest wall. She barely dared to breathe waiting for him to continue. 'What did you realise?' she said when he wouldn't tell her.

'That I care for you, Rosa. I just didn't want to admit it because I was afraid you might leave me.

When I heard about the accident today I thought I might lose you without ever telling you…'

'But why were you afraid I'd leave you?'

'Because my first wife did. Because she told me she loved me and she lied. Because she betrayed me, and I was scared it might happen again.'

'You thought I might *betray* you?'

He laughed. 'I know. It seems ridiculous. But I had to protect myself somehow. Not loving you—not admitting it—seemed the best way.'

She blinked up at him, wondering if he was really there, wondering if the drugs were giving her hallucinations and spinning stories that she wanted to hear. 'So what are you admitting?'

He took her free hand. 'I love you, Rosa. I'm sorry I made you sad. I'm sorry I ruined our wedding night. If I could make it up to you I would, a thousand times over.'

Tears pricked Rosa's eyes. 'Only one thousand?'

He smiled down at her and pressed his lips to hers before he said. 'Every night of our marriage. How does that sound instead?'

She smiled tremulously up at him. 'Much better. I love you so much, Vittorio.'

He gave a smile of wonderment then, as if he was exploring the new territory of these words and finding it to be everything he wanted and more. 'I love you, Rosa.'

They kissed just as the doctor bustled in.

'I'm so sorry to interrupt,' he said. 'Theatre is ready.'

'Don't be,' Vittorio said, smiling down at Rosa. 'We've got the rest of our lives to finish this.'

EPILOGUE

PRINCE GUGLIELMO ROBERTO D'MARBURG of Andachstein was born late one November morning, with a shock of black hair, a healthy set of lungs and weighing in at a very healthy four kilograms.

Measurements had been taken, paperwork completed, and the nursing staff had left now that the formalities were complete. Finally it was time for the new family to be left alone to bond.

Rosa relaxed into the pillows on the bed, her baby cradled in her arms, and leaned down to drink in his new baby breaths. 'He's so beautiful,' she said, her heart already swollen in size to accommodate this new love.

The baby yawned then, cracking open his eyes. 'Look,' she said. 'Blue eyes like sapphires. He's like a mini you.'

Vittorio sat by her side, one hand stroking his wife's still damp hair, the other under the arm holding their child, totally entranced.

'You were amazing,' he said to her. 'So strong.'

She shrugged, the pain of childbirth gone now that she was holding her reward. 'That's what women do. All around the world every day. It's not that special.'

'It's a miracle,' he said. 'Today I witnessed a miracle, performed by the woman I love.'

She smiled over at him. Things had been so different since her accident. Something had shifted in her warrior's hard and cynical heart, and the word he'd been most afraid to use and to hear was now a word she heard several times a day. And it would never grow old.

'Thank you,' she said. 'I love you, Vittorio.'

He lifted the closest of her hands and kissed it gently. 'And I love *you*. For this child you have given me. For just being you. But most of all I love you for loving me.'

Tears sprang from her eyes. Tears of joy.

'I made you cry,' he said, touching the pads of his forefingers to her eyes to wipe away the dampness.'

'Only because I'm so happy.'

'Then never stop crying,' he said, smiling. 'Thank you for rescuing me, Rosa. That day I found you lost by the bridge in Venice... I look back at that moment and I see...'

'Serendipity?' she offered.

'No,' he said. 'It was magic. Pure magic.'

And he leaned over and kissed the woman he loved.

* * * * *

If you enjoyed
Prince's Virgin in Venice
by Trish Morey,
You're sure to enjoy the other stories in our
Passion in Paradise collection!

Wedding Night Reunion in Greece
by Annie West
A Scandalous Midnight in Madrid
by Susan Stephens
His Shock Marriage in Greece
by Jane Porter

And why not explore these other
Trish Morey stories?

Shackled to the Sheikh
Consequence of the Greek's Revenge

Available now!